Secrets

IN

THE WIND

RUMKI CHOWDHURY

DJARABI KITABS PUBLISHING
Dallas, Texas
USA

For information contact:

DJARABI KITABS PUBLISHING

PO BOX 703733

DALLAS, TX 75370

www.djarabikitabs.com

Cover Design Concept by Rumki Chowdhury
Full Cover by Sam Rog
ISBN-13: 978-1-947148-63-5
Category & Genre: Young Adult/Thriller
Library of Congress Control Number: 9781947148611
First Print Edition: February 2023
10 9 8 7 6 5 4 3 2 1

ALSO BY RUMKI CHOWDHURY

DEDICATION

First and foremost, I am grateful to Allah for everything.

I dedicate this book to my three pearls, Amina, Maryam and Asiya,

who I pray may tread the path toward knowledge and become

exemplary human beings, Ameen.

CONTENTS

CHAPTER 1

THE WIND

I wore a pair of flat-heeled, brown sandals, which I could easily slip on and off when resting on our plane journey from JFK Airport in New York City to Dhaka Airport in Bangladesh. The most modest yet comfortable travel attire I could think of was a traditional *kurti*, similar to that of the top of a *salwar kameez*, only it was a knee-length top paired with skinny jeans instead of "Aladdin" pants. My kurti was embroidered with red and green threadwork of intricate floral patterns. *It's a perfect representation of the colors of*

2

the Bangladeshi flag, I thought to myself. I had hoped that in wearing these traditional clothes, I would make the perfect first impression on the people of Bangladesh after fifteen years of being away.

We almost missed our chance again. However, I insisted to my parents, whom I called *Amma* and *Abba* in Bengali, that it would be okay despite being in my last and most critical year of high school.

I forced myself to regain my balance within this imaginary Jenga game of SATs, college applications, college essays, scholarship applications, extracurricular activities, volunteer hours and so much more.

"This could be our last chance," I had explained to Amma and Abba. "Who knows what my schedule will look like when I'm in college?!"

The Jenga blocks almost toppled over, but I leaned against the wall as I said this.

"Okay, Asha," they replied, admitting they had already been looking at tickets.

"Madam, the seat belt sign is on," the flight attendant said, jarring me out of my flashback.

Turbulence carried us most of the journey and I closed my eyes, hoping-- praying for sleep. Instead, I found myself picking up *Frankenstein* by Mary Wollstonecraft Shelley, a book I chose to read and analyze for my AP English class. I flicked through the brightly colored sticky tabs I used to bookmark my analytical notes. Skimming through the pencil markings on one page, I silently read the words, *"It is true, we shall be monsters, cut off from the world, but on that account we shall be more attached to one another."* With that, I felt the plane take a violent dip in the air, causing me to drop the book. I took off my belt and quickly scooped it up.

"Why do you always read scary books?" Amma asked, pointing to the gruesome cover image.

"Because…they're entertaining… plus, there's a lot to learn from *Frankenstein*." I was obsessed with Gothic literature and any books that had to do with monsters and the supernatural. I flipped through the pages as I spoke. "The dichotomies are endless! There's good versus evil, truth versus lies, light versus darkness…." I looked up to see Amma had shut her eyes again. I stuck my tongue out at her.

"I saw that," she said.

Shrugging my shoulders, I continued skimming the quotes I had underlined until my thoughts drifted off toward what Amma had asked me. *Why do you always read scary books? Since we were little, we've been told scary stories about things that creep and crawl in the night to teach us some kind of a lesson or keep us from doing anything stupid,* I guessed.

Suddenly, I noticed the whistling of the wind breaking into a roar every time the pilot attempted to take control of the uncontrollable. I tried distracting myself by reading: *"Man! You may hate, but beware! Your hours will pass in dread and misery, and soon the bolt will fall which must ravish from you your happiness forever. Are you to be happy while I grovel in the intensity of my wretchedness? You can blast my other passions, but revenge remains...."*

Before I could finish reading the sentence, Amma snatched *Frankenstein* out of my hands and replaced it with a magazine. She then closed her eyes again and moved her lips silently in prayer as she held firmly onto her armrest.

I said a little prayer too. Then, I opened up the magazine. There was a printed image of a sad little girl standing in front of a vast wasteland. It was an ad asking for donations to a charity in Bangladesh. *Frankenstein* still on the brain, I imagined his large monstrous hand emerging from the garbage and pulling at the girl's hair. I could almost hear her screaming, but upon the pilot's words, "Ladies and

Gentleman, we have arrived at Dhaka Airport," I realized that what I *actually* heard was the screeching of the plane's wheels as it landed.

After exiting the airplane, we waited in a long line for our passports to be checked at the arrival gate. I continued reading *"--revenge, henceforth dearer than light or food! I may die, but first you, my tyrant and tormentor, shall curse the sun that gazes on your misery. Beware, for I am fearless and therefore powerful. I will watch with the wiliness of a snake, that I may sting with its venom. Man, you shall repent of the injuries you inflict."*

With that, I felt something wrap around my arm and squeeze it. Startled, I looked up to see that it was Amma's hand. When I made eye contact with her, she nodded in the direction of a middle-aged man, staring at us ...at me. I was about to ask him if he needed help with anything when Amma's fingers clawed deeper into my skin.

"Ouch," I shrieked and she loosened her grip a bit.

"I don't see anything wrong with asking the guy if he needs help!"

"How is it that at your age, you still don't understand stranger danger?!" She asked, rhetorically, of course.

Abba added, "Asha, your mother is right; you need to be careful around here; there are tigers lurking at every corner."

"Abba, if you mean *actual* Bengal tigers, they don't roam in *this* part of Bangladesh and they're an endangered species because it's *our* fault, not theirs."

We three looked over at the man again. A security officer handed him a cane and linked arms with him to lead him out.

"Blind tigers, eh?" I winced.

Meanwhile, Amma and Abba pretended not to hear me.

We handed over our passports for the security to check, grabbed our luggage from baggage claim, and were on our way out. We searched the crowd for familiar faces until I noticed a man, flowers in hand, walking straight toward us.

"I can't believe my eyes!" My uncle, whom I called *Khalu* in Bengali, stretched out his arm to present me with an ombre of lilies which I accepted. "Is this itty bitty Asha?"

"Er, not so itty bitty anymore, I hope," I replied before realizing my blood was being sucked by an army of mosquitos. I smacked my arms and hands.

"Ah, don't worry, *dengue fever* season is over!"

I widened my eyes at Khalu's comment. He just laughed and wrapped his long arms around me before moving on to greet my parents. "Hope you had a comfortable flight!" He said.

I was glad he didn't ask me how the flight went

exactly or I would have been forced to reply something along the lines of, the wind and air were vicious and vociferous, at which point we would have suffered an awkward silence between us.

"Welcome to Bangladesh, my beautiful niece!" My aunt, whom I called *Khala,* chimed in before hugging me. I thanked her. She was just two years younger than Amma. Her daughter, my cousin, Kushi, was 17 –years old, the same age as me. The last time I saw Kushi was when I was two –years old! Our trip from back then left me with no memory of it...only a 12" x 12" leather photo album to look back on and memorize. There weren't many photographs of my cousin in my album, though. However, I remembered one black and white photograph of us both wearing matching polka-dotted dresses. That was why when I noticed Khala looked so much like my mother, gray eyes and all, I wondered if Kushi had inherited their eye color because I certainly had not. On the contrary, I inherited my cinnamon complexion and the slight bump on my nose from Abba, whose name was Shah, meaning "king or emperor" in Bengali. His royal highness worked as a postman back in the USA; his blue uniform always brought out his big, brown eyes, another thing I got from him.

"Joyti, where's our beautiful niece?" Amma asked Khala.

She replied, "Sorry Amita, but Kushi has school, so she couldn't come. However, she is eager to see you all. Let's hurry!"

As we walked out, a blast of warm air surrounded me, tugging at the edge of my sleeves, at the hem of my kurti, and pulling the shawl off my head to play with my hair. It was as if I were some mythological creature subject to probing and experimentation. The Bangladeshi air simply did not recognize me nor did it seem to understand me.

We took a privately-hired car to the Dhaka Airport bus station. Khalu insisted on wheeling my luggage as we walked toward the bus ticket counter. On the way, I noticed a row of green buses.

"Nice, aren't they?" Khalu said. "Wait until you get inside. It's quite cozy with chairs that lean all the way back." The white and gray streaks on his beard came to life as he spoke. It was as if leaning chairs, alongside self-driving vehicles, were the latest innovation.

Abba asked him, "How long will the bus journey be, Nil?"

"About five to six hours, depending on traffic."

With that, Khalu shot his eyes toward the guy behind the bus ticket counter and demanded, "We want the very front seats and there better be no malfunctions with them. The chairs have to lean all the way back and have no scratches on the leather."

"Oh, we cannot guarantee that, Sir," replied the man over the counter in his most gentle and customer-friendly voice.

"We are not paying for uncertainties. You'd better send someone out there to check on the seats, or else you are going to see my wrath."

The man behind the counter began to fidget upon hearing Khalu's tone. His eyes wandered in search of the best possible answer when he spotted a small, young man wiping windows. He called upon the man and whispered something into his ear. Then, the young man wiped his hands dry, scurried out of the office and hopped onto a bus.

Having witnessed his commands being met, Khalu smirked. I was appalled, and he noticed. "This, my dear, is how you have to handle things in life, so you don't get screwed over."

Seated on the bus, I felt it quake before it drove off

with a loud vroom. We were on our way, slothfully alongside *CNGs* that looked like green boxes on three wheels and vibrant *rickshaws* that were like horse carriages, only smaller and ridden by mostly men in *lungis,* although I have read about women slowly rising to that role. Both forms of transportation had flowery patterns mottled all over them. They reminded me of decorated floats at a parade.

Amma sat next to me and leaned all the way back in her chair. "You can relax now, Asha. Take a nap. You barely slept during the plane journey," she said.

Her words pulled my jaw open. "I'm about to experience scenic Bangladesh, and you expect me to sleep?!"

Amma had already dozed off into dreamland. I leaned my head against the large bus window. After a short while, the bus cruised onto the dusty and uneven highway.

Sitting upright, I admired the jade tea gardens and

the golden rice fields, both filled with men and women laboring away. The fishermen, with their pointy straw hats and standing up inside their canoes, tossed nets into the water. I saw cow herders striding alongside cows. The village children lightly tapped black and white goats with branches, perhaps to guide them in the right direction. Chickens, roosters and their chicks waddled around mint-green houses protected by rooftops made of tin. *It must sound like an opening night at a Broadway musical on the roof when it rains*, I thought to myself.

We stopped at a gas station for fuel, restroom use and a snack break. Salesmen balanced large fruit baskets on their heads. I wondered how they managed to walk, so poised, from vehicle to vehicle, selling their goods through passenger windows. Near our bus, an old man sold peanuts and a teenager sold *achar:* yummy and gooey dried fruit turned into balls of sour and sweet delights. They can also be different types of pickled fruits or vegetables. I was about to hand the boy some money when Amma smacked my hand away. *She* handed him the money.

"Another dangerous…I mean, *endangered* Bengal tiger?" I asked her. She ignored me before dozing off again.

"Don't eat too much of that, or you'll get a stomach ache," Abba said.

"I popped anti-diarrhea tablets just in case," I said, wiping my hands with a wet wipe and spraying on hand sanitizer before digging in.

Khala bought a packet of peanuts and offered some to me. I cracked open the soft shell to find not two but three nuts, all lined in a row, inside. They tasted rich and sweet.

Along the road, there was a row of bazaars featuring large posters of gorgeous models adorned by jewelry and intricately-designed sarees, beckoning me to write up a shopping list.

Amma, who had trouble sleeping during our bumpy and noisy journey, noticed the lust in my eyes. "Shopping can wait until we reach Sylhet," she said.

As we continued our bus journey, with my parents, aunt and uncle trying to sleep in chairs (that "leaned all the way back"), my best companion had been, in fact, Bangladesh. We had only begun getting to know one another. It would take time before we could understand each other. I felt around inside my bag to take out my journal, but I blindly took out *Frankenstein* instead. I looked over at Amma, who seemed too tired to complain about it. *That is one horrific book cover!* I suddenly realized and tucked it safely back into my bag. I then took out my journal, which I dubbed "My Little Tanzanite" after a precious and rare gem that I researched once in science class. With internet access nonexistent on the bus, I decided to write down my feelings which I would later transfer onto my blog:

I feel hesitation in the land's breath every time it puffs at me.
I see the questions curved upward in its eyebrows. I see its lips quiver
every time it smiles back at me. We are still strangers, but my goal is
to part as friends...perhaps, the best of friends.

I closed my eyes and let coconut palms whisper their secrets to me, but before I could decipher them, there was a loud "Pang!"

The bus driver almost crashed into a CNG. "Hey!" He shouted. "You wanna get yourself killed or something?!" Although, I couldn't help but wonder if the CNG driver should have been the one asking that question considering the difference in vehicle size. He continued driving and so did the CNG, toward their allocated destinations. No police reports. Not even an apology! Meanwhile, I felt like the bus driver owed *me* an apology! Who did he think he was, recklessly driving?! His actions skulked into my head and stole me away from the sweet sound of the coconut palms, dancing and singing in the breeze!

The bus began to viciously sway from side-to-side as if on a race track. Through the large window in front of the driver, I saw the reason why. He was driving on the wrong side of the road. Oncoming traffic posed the inevitable threat of an accident. I recited my prayer, *"Inna lillahi wa inna ilaihi rajiwoon,"* which Muslims recite in Arabic when experiencing a tragedy or hearing of someone's death. It means, "From God we came and to God we shall return."

I spent those last three hours gripping onto the edge of my seat. My nails probably tore apart the pristine leather that my uncle had fought so hard for us to sit on.

I tried to force my eyes off the wretched road in front of me and back onto the pristine window, on my side. I imagined how it felt with the essence of the wind washing over the bus, every bit of green that knocked on my window, the movement of labor and hard work, all of which were lyrically pieced together and sounded wholly in-tune in my head. Then, I felt a sudden jerk.

"Sylhet!" the driver called out. I released my sweaty palms from my seat. On my way out, I narrowed my eyes at him as if to say, *you almost killed us; the least you can do is apologize!* As I stepped off the bus, I wondered what the coconut palms had whispered to me and whether or not I would hear them again. *Were they calling on me to visit them? Were they welcoming me to Bangladesh? Were they asking me questions about life in the USA?*

The last thought took me back to the night before we set off for JFK Airport. I had been sitting on my mauve pink desk chair in our Bronx apartment and was blogging about how ecstatic I was about our trip:

The closest I had ever been to seeing my Bengali culture was opening up Amma's wardrobe and admiring the vast array of sarees and salwar kameezes, in every color and in every nyans of those colors.

The closest I had ever been to smelling and tasting my culture were the blend of spices Amma and Abba cooked into their curries. The closest I had ever been to feeling my culture was the henna Amma adorned my hands with on special occasions like the Muslim holiday of Eid-Ul-Fitr, celebrating the end of the fasting month of Ramadan. The closest I had ever been to hearing my culture was the poetry and stories Abba read out loud to me from his collection of Bengali literature.

Finally, finally...I will be experiencing my culture, bathing in The Surma River, walking on its cobblestones and dirt roads, picking and eating the fruits off of its trees, buying traditional street food and basking under the sunrise and sunset, both times of which the sun is crimson. The sun is as red as the very blood of the martyrs that had fought to preserve our Bengali culture in 1971.

After having completed the draft, I took out one of my childhood photos from my last visit to Bangladesh. In the photograph, I was wearing a yellow dress with a matching summer hat on my head; my father held me as my mother rested her hand on his shoulder; we were sitting in front of a row of red, yellow and white tulips at a park. I scanned and uploaded the photograph and published my blog entry. With that, I closed my computer and took in a deep breath, imagining the adventures Amma, Abba and I were about to experience.

"Welcome home," Khalu said, waking me up to the *reality* of the beginning of our adventures.

Home. There I was, taking in another deep breath, seeing it all before my eyes. A brisk wind brushed against my shoulders as I exhaled and I held onto that wind, my hand clutching my shoulder, my eyes closed, my head tilted upward toward the red sun, letting its rays cleanse me. I felt like I belonged there, whether or not the Bangladeshi land and air had accepted me yet. After all, my name means "hope" in the Bengali language and holding onto *asha*, I whispered to the land and air, "We will become friends... I just know it."

But I spoke too soon. As we walked through the large white gates and up the pathway, I tripped over a cobblestone and nearly fell. I caught myself and my bag, but *Frankenstein* splurged out onto the pathway. Khalu picked it up, but he didn't hand it to me right away. Instead, he opened the book, flipped through the pages and skimmed a few of my pencil markings.

"English class," I said with a nervous smile as if I hadn't chosen it... but I *had*. He was too busy reading my pencil markings to notice my smile. I wondered what Khalu was thinking about the words I had underlined. I wondered what Khalu was thinking about *me,* as a person, based on the kind of books I read.

He just scrunched his eyebrows, made a *hmph* sound and finally handed *Frankenstein* back to me. The book was still wide open and I couldn't help but read the words that Khalu most probably noticed: *"Devil," I exclaimed, "do you dare approach me? And do not you fear the fierce vengeance of my arm wreaked on your miserable head? Begone, vile insect! Or rather, stay, that I may trample you to dust!"*

"Don't be shy, Asha," Khala said. "As long as you are here, this is your home."

With that, I shut *Frankenstein,* stuffed it back into my bag and walked in.

CHAPTER 2

FEAR

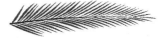

The smell of chai, with its mix of cardamoms and cinnamon, lured me into a grand living room. The floors beneath my feet were marble and rich, glistening. There was a lot of wooden furniture, some of which outlined rich textiles. There were two servants awaiting our arrival, Zulekha and her husband, Abdul. Zulekha wore an orange *saree,* which was a piece of cloth, usually 5 to 6 yards long, and wrapped as elegantly as possible around a woman's body. Abdul wore a lungi and a white shirt. They had been working for Khala and Khalu for many years.

After introductions, Khala said, "Take their things to their bedrooms."

"Look at how big you have grown!" Zulekha said. She hugged me.

Khala frowned at this and pulled me away. She was obviously not used to people hugging their servants or vice versa; I heard it was like an unspoken rule not to touch each other so much, an ultimate breach of class differences or social decorum.

Zulekha took my luggage and said, "When you were just a toddler, I used to fry you chips and do pigtails in your hair." Her smile was so wide I spotted a chipped tooth in one of the corners. Her hair was combed back into an updo, and she wore a golden nose ring. *So cool, I wonder if I should get one, too, while I'm here.*

There was a luxurious work of tapestry on the floor.

Khala sat me down on cozy cushions on the intricately-carved wooden chairs. I had imagined her to be chubbier and to have wrinkles creeping across her face, as is common among women her age. However, she was surprisingly glowing with a wide and toothy smile underneath her pointy nose and in between her smooth cheeks. Her figure had, however, grown slimmer with age. On the contrary, Khalu´s age showed on his beard and on his round belly.

I asked her what her *fountain of youth* was.

"Coconuts," she answered as if the answer should have been obvious. "I drink the water, eat them, and I put coconut oil in my hair every night before I sleep."

As if I knew it all along, I said, "Of course, coconuts." *Was that the secret the coconut palms were trying to share with me?*

After an exchange of conversation between my parents, my aunt, my uncle, and myself about the home decor and lifestyle of Bangladesh, a glorious plate of warm and toasty *shingaras* appeared on top of the coffee table before me. It was Abdul who had made and served those tasty bundles of pastries with potato filling.

"Thank you! They look delicious!"

"Anything for you, Dear. Do you remember who I am?"

Abdul was a thinly-built and chocolate-toned man in his forties with tints of silver on his *Charlie Chaplin* mustache.

"No, sorry." *I was only two!*

"I used to tell you bedtime stories and give you piggyback rides."

"Well, then, you will have to tell me a story tonight," I said.

He chuckled. Abdul was just about to reply when Khala interrupted.

"Go make rice. This girl needs some *real* food after the journey she just had." With that, Abdul scurried out. I looked at the shingaras, saliva building up around my tongue and gums. I grabbed one and gulped it down before asking, "Where is Kushi, by the way? You said she would be waiting for us?" I nearly spit out bits of my savory snack as I spoke.

One might wonder why my aunt and uncle, like my parents, only had one child when most Bengali families extended to as many as five or more! Regardless, I never got bored of being an only child because I was always around family, whether in the USA or abroad. Not to mention, my extended family reached *as far as* and continued to expand *like* the universe. I was looking forward to meeting the ones in Bangladesh.

"Are you home, Kushi?" Khala called out to her daughter.

"Yes, Amma!"

In came this flamingo of a human being. Kushi was taller than the average Bengali girl, with a long neck and the grace of royalty. I noticed her long, flowy and silky brunette hair, matching her hazel eyes. Her complexion was as golden as honey and glistened like amber. Her light blue school uniform was that of a salwar kameez with a white shawl draped over her neck. She wore platform sandals, the straps intricately embroidered with petite white pearls. Her smile was radiant. She was glorious, and I couldn't stop staring as she greeted my parents with "Salam," a Muslim greeting that means *peace* in Arabic.

"You must be Asha," she said.

I stuck out my hand so that we could shake hands. She threw her arms around me, instead, bending down considering our height difference.

"Nice to meet you," I mumbled into her neck. She smelled like *attar,* an essential oil used for fragrance.

30

"You have no idea how excited I was when I heard you were coming! And now that you're here, I can't believe it!"

"Me too!" I genuinely beamed a corner-to-corner smile.

"Food is ready," Zulekha called out. We saw the table adorned with an assortment of different curries, mango achar and of course, white rice.

"Come, let's eat," Kushi said, grabbing my hand and pulling me softly from the living room to the dining room. She insisted that we sit together. We talked about and compared our favorite movies, what kind of books we read, our studies, school routines and of course, shopping. We made plans on what we would do together, where she wanted to take me. We had a lot in common.

"I am so excited to practice my English with you!" Kushi said. "It's my favorite subject at school!"

31

She spoke it well, too. Her vocabulary was impeccable for someone who spoke English as a second language.

"I try to read books in the English language and I read your blog, too," Kushi blurted.

"Really?"

She nodded. "When Amma told me about your blog, I knew I had to look it up. I'm officially hooked! Your choice of wording is so poetic and inspiring."

Poetic and inspiring. I let those words sink in a little. After all, it was coming from a fan. *Be humble!*

"Your mom read it too?"

"Oh, yes. Khala always brags about your writing and how smart you are. She's really proud of you," Kushi said, referring to Amma.

After the meal, I went upstairs to freshen up and change from my kurti and pants into a more comfortable

32

kaftan, a loose maxi dress worn by many cultures, including Moroccans and South Asians.

As soon as I opened the door, I was startled to see Abdul standing there.

"Sorry to scare you, Dear," he said after seeing me gasp. "Your khala insisted that I bring you a glass of warm milk before you go to sleep."

"Oh, thank you, Abdul. You really shouldn't have!"

"Actually, I should. It's my job."

"Right…." I took a sip of the milk, and as if some potion, it made me automatically close my eyes and drift off for a bit.

"Would you like me to tell you a story?" His words forced my eyes open.

He smiled in a hopeful way, and despite my feeling exhausted from my journey from the Bronx to Sylhet, I replied, "Mhm, okay, yes."

He took a few steps backward so that I could exit my room and go into the hallway, where there was a sofa for me to sit on and a coffee table to put my milk down.

"Where's Kushi? Isn't she going to join us?" I asked.

"Kushi, madam, is studying for exams."

Madam? I just nodded, taking another sip of my milk.

"This is a true story about your mother when she was a child. I know about it because we all grew up in the same village together. But, I have to warn you, it's scary, and seeing as it's night time ...."

"Are you kidding me? I LOVE scary stories! ESPECIALLY at night time. ESPECIALLY real ones! You know what would have made this storytime even better?"

Abdul shook his head.

"If we were sitting outside, under the night sky and

34

the trees, and around a campfire!"

He seemed a bit unsure of how to respond, so he gave me a firm nod and left momentarily. By the time he returned, I had gulped down my milk. Zulekha followed him in. Each person carried two pots of plants and placed them as close to me as they could. I was basically surrounded by four large plants at hands-reach.

"Is this good?" She asked me.

I nodded, wondering if that was some sort of storytelling ritual I was unfamiliar with...*plants*....

Zulekha sat down on the carpet, legs folded. Abdul lit a candle and placed it on the coffee table in front of me. Then, he dimmed the hallway lights before joining Zulekha on the carpet.

"How is that?" He asked me and I finally understood that they were trying to recreate the outdoors, night sky and fire for me, except *indoors*.

"This is perfect, thank you," I replied.

"As a child, your mother had this habit of sleepwalking and sleeptalking. Does she still do that?" Abdul asked.

"Hmm…not sure about the sleepwalking, but she does mumble in her sleep," I replied.

"Well, one night, your mother was sleepwalking and found herself under a banyan tree near her school. When she looked up at the tree, she instantly fell to the ground, unconscious.

"Her father, your *nana*, found her and carried her back home. He put her in her bed and recited a few prayers from the Quran before throwing water on her face. Your nana and *nanu* thought that she might have seen something…some creature that could have possessed her! Some neighbors heard what had happened and immediately came by to support in any way they could. When your

36

mother woke up, she just whispered something and went back to sleep. Immediately, your *nana*, *nanu* and some neighbors saw a shadow creep out of the window. It was tall and had sharp, long nails. The next morning, your mother told us about some nightmare she had, where she saw a dark creature in a banyan tree, dangling its feet down from a branch before jumping down on top of her head. None of us told her that it was all real, but the people in the village were talking about it. Your mother overheard one of those conversations and confronted your nana and nanu. They explained that they didn't want to tell her in case the creature fed off her fear and came back to repossess her."

"And this was *real*? Like...it *really* happened to Amma?"

Abdul and Zulekha nodded.

"And you all believe that creatures, things that creep and crawl in the night, exist?"

"Of course we do! Don't you?" Abdul asked, as if it was more ridiculous for me *not* to believe in them than it was for me to actually believe in them.

The woman who had raised me and mocked me for reading too many scary stories had been a victim of horror, herself! I planned on confronting Amma about it, but first...*sleep*. Abdul and Zulekha fixed everything back to how it was in the hallway while I drowsily walked back to my room.

The house was a mansion with many rooms. In fact, I had to open about five doors before I discovered Kushi sitting at a dressing table with her brush in one hand and her phone in the other. As soon as I walked in, she slammed her phone down on the table. Then, she let out a sigh of relief.

"Oh, it's just you," she said. "Come in, come in!"

"I am so sorry, I didn't mean to startle you or barge

in like this. Your house is so big and…."

"Oh, feel free to barge in anytime, Sis."

Sis. It sounded so alien to me, but it sounded nice. We might just become like sisters. I wondered if I should call her "Sis," too. She sat down on her bed, which was covered by vibrant flower-mottled bedsheets.

Her phone buzzed and she, also in a kaftan, jumped at the sound.

"Never heard your phone vibrate before?"

"Um…I just wasn't expecting any messages."

"You must have a lot of friends?"

"Not really, just the best one. Her name is Zamila. Tell me about your friends. What are they like?"

"There's Rachel, Angel, Maria and Noreen. Rachel is a professional cyclist, Angel is a computer whiz, possibly a hacker, but that's unconfirmed. Maria is a Spanish beauty and she loves spicy food like us Bengalis. When she comes over, there is no need for Amma to cook anything catered to the average, non-adventurous human being. Noreen is Pakistani-American, so we have a lot in common, culture-wise.

"Wow, you're popular!" Kushi said with widened eyes.

"No, I'm not. I just have a few good friends. Tell me about your BFF; will I get to meet this...?"

"Zamila. She and I practically grew up together and went to the same schools as long as I can remember. She and I have a lot in common except that she's prettier." Kushi giggled. I joined her.

"You're gorgeous!"

"Look who's talking!"

I could get used to this. I wonder if we'll ever experience a sibling rivalry at this rate. I hear those can be brutal.

There is a sudden rumble outside. It sounded like a

motorcycle. Kushi gasped upon hearing it.

"What? You live in a country made for motorcycles and you're shocked by the noise?"

"Shh…." She eyed the window behind her dressing table. We watched shadows move across the walls as the headlight of a vehicle passed by.

I could see our reflection in the closed window. As I analyzed it, I noticed Kushi's eyes were so wide that her pupils seemed smaller. Her flawlessly-lined eyebrows curved upward. Her lips trembled. Something was off, and it had to do with whatever was outside of the house.

We heard a rumble, the sound of a motorcycle, like some phantom, disappearing in the distance, further down the road. As its rumble became a low buzzing noise like that of a mosquito's, I suddenly noticed that my cousin's grasp on my hand grew less and less tight. I was so taken by her facial expression in her reflection that I didn't even notice when she had grabbed my hand in the first place. She then patted my hand as if to say, *it's okay, but why wouldn't we be okay?* I saw the whites of my knuckles slowly revive into their cinnamon complexion. I looked up at my cousin. Her eyes were fixated on my hand as if she didn't want to look at me. I was left wondering whether she didn't *want* to look at me for fear that I would then be able to read her eyes…see what was wrong with her. In reality, she had no idea that I had already read her eyes… in her reflection, but had no idea what was wrong with her. My cousin had been jumpy the moment I walked in, the moment her phone vibrated, and the moment a motorcycle *zoomed* by.

I wanted so badly to ask her to open up to me. *What happened? Why did you feel the need to shush me? Why did we need to be quiet at the sound of a motorcycle? Why did you grab my hand and not let go until it disappeared? Why the fear-stricken facial expression?* Most of all, I wanted to ask her, *Are you in danger?*

Instead, I asked her, "What just happened?"

Finally meeting my eyes, struggling to smile, she answered, "I just get a little jumpy... when there's noise...like *that*."

"You were born and raised here. You live in a country that is overpopulated, over 160 million people, according to my research, where about 600,000 of them ride motorcycles! Judging from the traffic we just passed to get here, it's insane! This whole country is noisy and you're telling me you get a little jumpy at hearing *that* specific noise? Do you get why I have a hard time believing your excuse?"

"You did your research before traveling here?"

"Population, yes. Motorcycles, I researched traffic and vehicles when we got to your house because we almost had an accident today on the road."

"Oh no, are you okay?"

"I'm here, aren't I? Sitting on my cousin's bed,

trying to have an honest, open conversation with her, but I know all she's doing is avoiding answering my questions."

With that, she turned her back toward me, and looked at the window again. I got up, put my hand on her shoulder as a means of comfort for the sister I never had, for the sister I could have if only she would let me in. Silence hung over us, on top of the flaps of the ceiling fan, to be exact.

"I'm tired," she said.

"Me too, but just so you know, I'm here for you if you ever need to talk... about anything. Good night."

I waited for her to say it back to me, but she just stood there, statuesque, as if any movement she made at that moment, in front of her window, would have deemed her a target... for what, I had no idea. I wasn't even sure she had heard me.

As I was about to touch the doorknob, I heard

shuffling on the other side of it. Through the little space beneath the door, I noticed a shadow of someone. Two knocks thumped like thunder on the door. I turned around to see a petrified Kushi again. She shook her head, mouthing *No*.

I couldn't take it anymore, feeling like a prisoner in her room. "Tell me who this is!" I commanded.

"Abdul, Kushi Madam."

I looked at Kushi. She sat down on her bed with her hands on her chest, relieved.

I opened the door. Abdul had another glass of milk, this time for Kushi.

"Is Kushi Madam asleep?"

"No, I can take that for her." I closed the door and handed the glass to Kushi, who accepted it with shaky hands.

"Thank you," she said.

After she drank all of her milk, I asked her, "Feeling better?"

She nodded.

"Okay," I said and walked back toward the door.

"Asha," she said. I turned around, hoping she would tell me something…any little secret because I heard that's the kind of thing sisters share with one another. "Do you want to go shopping with me tomorrow?" She asked.

Even though that wasn't what I had expected her to say, I remained hopeful. "I'd love to, Sis."

Logic told me that we were cousins, yes, but that relation was not enough to build a relation*ship*. We barely knew each other. I had to earn her trust. Perhaps, we needed to rub coconut oil into each other's scalps; maybe, we needed to give each other makeovers or braid each other's hair; perhaps, we needed to just sit in silence, together, and listen to the coconut palms. Perhaps a girls' day out was just the kind of thing we needed to do.

That night, before I fell asleep, I faced the triple threat of nightmares I knew were coming for me: creatures hidden behind the leaves of banyan trees, my cousin's fear-stricken face and, of course, *Frankenstein.* I stared at the book cover while asking one question, *What or rather, WHO is the source of my cousin's fear?*

CHAPTER 3

THE BAZAAR

I thought about my conversation with Amma about getting a nose ring.

"You know, I used to have a nose ring," she said.

"Really?"

"Yup. Poked that hole in all by myself."

"DIY? So cool! Could you do that to my nose?"

"No, *Shuna*. Not worth the risk. It's best to let the professionals do it." Amma sometimes called me "shuna," the word for "gold" in Bengali.

"So...I *can* get a nose ring?"

"Sure, why not?!"

Ecstatic, I practically squeezed the life out of her. I wanted to return to America with a bang, and what better way to do that than with a nose ring?! *Eek, my friends are going to freak out!*

On the day I had planned on actually getting that nose ring, I looked into my reflection in the dresser mirror in the guest bedroom in Kushi's house. Then, I picked up my eyeliner and dabbed a black dot on my nose, where the nose ring would go. Satisfied, I brushed my frizzy hair into its otherwise straight, charcoal-black self. As I did this, I thought about how my mother, on the other hand, had wavy hair and milky skin and she looked amazing in almost anything except that neon school bus driver's vest she wore to work back in the Bronx. It washed her out. Her eyes, however, were striking no matter what she wore. They usually made people gawk at her, followed by the comment, "You don't look Bengali," because stereotypically, all Bengalis were "brown-skinned" and "dark-eyed." Then, those same people gave me that quizzical look...I imagined they were questioning whether or not I had been adopted.

I took a good look in the mirror and analyzed my facial features. I had the shape of my mother's face and the shape of her eyes and the shape of her lips. It comforted me, not because I was questioning whether or not she *was*, indeed, my mother and I, her daughter. Rather, it comforted me knowing that all of my life, whenever I would miss her, I could look into the mirror and somehow *see* her.

With that thought, I wiped away the dot on my nose and patted my face dry with a towel. I then wore a simple, white, lace *salwar kameez* and grabbed my black leather purse before leaving the guest bedroom. Kushi had suggested that we scour the shops. My mother and aunt had other plans, visiting a cousin who lived nearby. As I walked down the corridor, I told myself to hurry up before Amma caught me. She would have been an excellent FBI agent as she was capable of reading my slightest gesture, my eyes...and knowing almost immediately my most inner thoughts.

As I reached the staircase, I heard a voice calling out to me from behind. Almost tripping, I caught myself by grabbing the railing. I patted down my hair and my outfit, repositioned the bag over my shoulder, and turned around as gracefully as I could manage.

"Yes, Amma?" I sang in the sweetest note possible. *Do not show a hint of anything that happened with Kushi the night before, Asha*, I told myself.

Amma wore a flower-printed kaftan, and her hair was up in a messy bun. She had a hairbrush in her hand. I decided to focus my eyes on that, the exact tactic Kushi tried on me the night before, but that's the thing about X-Rays; you have to face them one way or another.

"Are you in such a hurry that you couldn't even say 'goodbye' to your own mother?"

"I thought you had left already."

"No, I'm taking my time, as should you. We're on vacation, you know?"

Don't look her in the eyes, Asha!

"Thank you for the advice. I will be off now. Goodbye."

"Look at me," she commanded.

I looked up...at her chin.

"Meet my eyes," she demanded in her *mom*-tone. "Come closer."

She might as well have thrown a rope around me and pulled me closer.

In other words, I obeyed.

"Now," she briskly positioned my hair behind my shoulders. "What's wrong?"

"Nothing's wrong. Why would anything be wrong?" I blurted out the words as fast as a high-speed train heading for a train wreck.

"You're not allowed to leave until you tell me." She crossed her arms to show me that she meant it.

"But Kushi is waiting."

"She will have to wait...as long as it takes."

I rolled my eyes. She shot me her most intimidating look, which coerced me into walking toward the guest bedroom where she and my father slept the night before. "Are you nervous about getting a nose ring?" She asked.

"Yes, exactly," I answered.

"Why do I sense there's more?"

You know, the ear piercing instrument thingy...and I remember that it hurts a bit...a lot, actually...yeah."

"As a little girl, you pet a snake at the zoo. Not to mention, you read haunting books! I'm not buying any of this!"

Train wreck!

Once we were both inside the bedroom, I shut the door behind us and said, "There's something wrong with Kushi. I don't know what it is. She won't tell me. All I know is that last night when we were in her bedroom, her phone vibrated, which is normal; phones vibrate, but it obviously made Kushi nervous.

Then, there was a motorcycle passing by her window and she was just so...so afraid...like someone was after her or something."

"Did you ask her what was wrong?"

"Yes, like I said, she wouldn't tell me.

I guess we're just getting to know one another, and I have to earn her trust. Could you, maybe...."

"Speak to my sister and try to get some information?" My mother interjected, reading my mind and finishing off my sentence.

X-Ray vision. Total FBI-agent.

"Yes, without telling her what I just informed you. You'll have better luck figuring out what's happening as you're both sisters, and you probably tell each other everything."

"Okay, I'll speak with her even though I think you may be overreacting, and Kushi is probably just fine."

"If it was me, you wouldn't be saying that."

"What do you mean?"

"You, who keep warning me about tigers lurking in the shadows, are not worried about Kushi at all?"

"Well…she *was* born and raised here."

"Ah, so it's nature versus nurture, where she is equipped to handle those kinds of attacks, right? Kind of…

like you were equipped to handle them?"

"Me? What are you talking about?"

So, I told her about the creatures that crept and crawled in the night and how I heard that she had been attacked by one.

She released a long sigh and said nothing.

"Can I go now?" I asked, breaking the dead air.

"Of course, have fun! Try not to think too much about Kushi's situation."

"I'll try. Salam!"

"Oh and Asha!"

"Yes?" I asked through gritted teeth.

"You and Kushi will get there, too."

"Get where?"

"Where you tell each other everything. Just...give it time." I nodded. With that, I ran down the stairs and out of the house, my heart knocking against my rib cage, begging me to release it into the horizon and embrace the rays of the sun.

Woof, woof, woof! A stray dark dog barked at me from across the street. I hopped into the CNG vehicle Kushi had arranged for us.

I got inside only to see we were matching. Kushi also wore white, a cotton salwar kameez with turquoise threadwork along the hemline, neckline and sleeves. The square neckline design accentuated her long neck, making her seem even taller.

There were no seat belts nor doors to this three-wheeled vehicle a.k.a "tuk tuk" or "auto rickshaw."

It zoomed off so quickly I thought I would fall out of it. I held on tightly to the seat.

The sound of the engine was deafening.

"What does CNG stand for?" I had to yell over the sound.

"Compressed natural gas," Kushi yelled back. "It's supposed to be less harmful to the environment. Causes the least amount of pollution."

I noticed she was even quieter than she had been the night before. That was the first time she really spoke to me all morning and it was only to answer a question. Breakfast was silent; our thoughts floated around as our parents chatted away about their childhood memories, how they used to celebrate the Muslim holiday of Eid, how their parents taught them to swim by using a log for support, and then just throwing them into the water. *Talk about survival of the fittest!* I once asked Kushi to pass me the butter, and that, too, she did in silence.

I was surprised no one else at the table noticed how quiet she had been, at least not enough to get suspicious about it. *Not even Amma. Maybe, she only has that X-Ray vision on me because I'm her daughter?*

The dust particles from the dirt road tickled my nose and throat. I took an allergy tablet, but I was afraid it wouldn't be powerful enough, and my allergies would get exasperated during the journey. However, the journey didn't last too long and my allergy medication seemed to be working.

"Where are we going?" I asked yet another question, hoping to keep a conversation going this time.

"The bazar's not far. Just a few more minutes. It's the traffic that really slows us down here. But, of course, you'd know that from your research, right?"

I narrowed my eyes at her because I did not like the tone with which she asked me that rhetorical question.

We came to a roundabout; cars, rickshaws, CNG's zigzagged in different directions; the sound of shouting and horns honking was like an angry mob enclosing us. When we came onto the main shopping road, a little boy, wearing only pants and ripped sandals, chased our vehicle while yelling, "Londoni Madam, Londoni Madam, some money, please, help us, money, money, money!"

Kushi yelled back in Bengali, "We aren't Londoni, we are Bangladeshi."

"Listen," *she* was starting a conversation with me for the *first* time today. "Do *not* give any money to the poor kids on the streets here until we are sitting in a CNG again on our way back home."

"Why not before that?"

"Because once you give one kid money, the rest swarm in. You might not spot them now, but they're all hidden in different locations, and they're...like ducks. You throw bread for one of them to eat, and the rest follow, and before you know it, you run out of money, leaving some of them disappointed. And that's not the worst part; they will run after you, asking you for more, unwilling to accept that you have nothing left in your bag; you will then feel guilty for not bringing enough money."

"Ah, I see," I replied. "That's why we don't do it until we are sitting in a CNG again, ready to drive off and escape the inevitable disappointment on the little ones' faces and the inevitable guilt in my heart."

Kushi frowned and nodded.

The CNG swerved sharply, and I flew onto Kushi. As the driver kept going, we heard a scream in the distance behind us.

"What just happened?!" Kushi asked. I sat back up and slid across to my side of the CNG. My body was quaking, a reaction of the aftermath.

"We almost crashed into a *rickshaw*, madam," the driver answered. "Drive carefully! You'll kill us!" Kushi said before she warned, "And my father is a renowned architect. He won't spare you if he hears of my death!"

That moment reminded me of how Khalu spoke to the bus customer service near Dhaka Airport: *This, my dear, is how you have to handle things in life, so you don't get screwed over.*

I noticed through the mirror that the CNG driver grew tight-mouthed.

Then, I looked over at Kushi.

"You are your father's daughter," I said.

"Huh?"

"Nothing." I picked my shoulders up before dropping them again.

The way the wind blew through Kushi's hair made her look ethereal. Meanwhile, I looked into the car mirror and noticed my hair getting frizzy due to the humidity. It just floated in static motion like inside a plasma nebula ball.

"Do you have a driver's license?" I asked her.

She didn't reply. I noticed she hadn't heard me.

I yelled over the engine noise, "Do you have a driver's license?"

"Who, me?" She yelled back. "You were talking to me? Sorry, I thought you were asking our driver."

I giggled. "So...do you?"

"I might get one in the near future, but I doubt I will be driving so much in packed areas like these."

"I wouldn't either if I were you. My dad taught me how to drive, so I'm currently on the provisional license and will get my official one when I turn 18 next month."

"Oh, that's so exciting! I turn 18 in six months." She frowned and shrugged her shoulders as the CNG stopped. "Ah, we're here!"

We both stuck our hands in our bags, but Kushi insisted on paying the driver.

"You're my guest; you're not allowed to pay." She smiled warmly.

I thought about how I had already seen so many sides to Kushi up to that point. I saw the friendly Kushi, Kushi my blog fan, the fear-stricken Kushi, the annoyed Kushi, and the warm Kushi.

After she paid the driver, we made our way through a crowd and into what looked like my closet with its array of colors, except 50 times bigger!

I was in the midst of the most luscious aroma of fabrics, each one soaring in the air and landing back onto the sellers' counters, screaming for attention and begging to be adopted.

Each seller we passed called us to come over and see what they had in their store for us. Kushi seemed to know her way around, so I just followed closely behind. She even held my hand so as not to lose me.

"Come on, Sis, let's make our way to meet my friend, Zamila."

"Oh, that's exciting!" *Did she just call me "Sis" again?*
Maybe today, I can finally earn her trust. Shopping is an opportunity
for the ultimate sisterly bonding time!

"Yeah! Zamila is likable, and so are you; I'm sure
you will get along just fine."

"*Chaatpoti?*" She asked, pointing to an outside
counter where two men served a pot of chickpeas cooked
into a sauce. I decided to be adventurous and try it.

As I scooped up the first spoon, my tastebuds
screamed *Fire, fire, save me!* Yet, I could not resist taking more
spoonfuls of this delicious yet fiery delicacy. I took a break
in between to wipe my runny nose, an instant reaction to
the hotness of chaatpoti.

Kushi watched me and laughed. "It's so spicy,
right?"

"Yeah, but I can't stop eating it. It's so good!" I
struggled to say in between deep breaths.

Out of nowhere, a motorcyclist with a helmet appeared. Kushi dropped her spoon, startled and anticipating something. As soon as the motorcyclist took off his helmet, Kushi looked immediately relieved.

"Is everything okay?" I asked her.

She showed me her empty bowl. "Perfect!"

The man over the counter gave us two glasses of milk, which we gulped down at once.

We then climbed a narrow staircase up to a glass door. Pushing it open, we smelled the continuous perfume of freshly-designed fabrics. Sitting behind one of the counters was a girl who looked around our age. She had the curliest hair I had ever seen and a pink, flower-printed salwar kameez. Her skin was glowing beneath the store lights. Kushi hugged her.

"Zamila, meet my cousin, Asha."

Zamila threw her arms around me and whispered, "Welcome to Bangladesh."

"Thank you so much."

"So…," she stretched out her arms wide enough, gesturing toward the rainbow of fabrics. "See anything you like?"

"Everything here is so beautiful; I wouldn't know where to start."

"Take your time." Zamila walked back behind a counter. "I'm also here to help."

Noticing curiosity riddled all over my face, Kushi said, "Zamila's parents own this shop. I am a loyal customer and my mom, your khala, insists on *our* gifting you with an outfit today. It's on us."

"No, no, I couldn't accept. That's too much."

"If you don't like anything here, we can always go to another shop."

"I'd be a tad bit offended, though," Zamila whispered.

"No, no, it's not that. You really don't have to give me anything," I insisted. "I appreciate just spending time together with you."

"But we insist on the gift so accept it, or you will break some hearts today...including mine, Sis." Kushi smirked as I hung onto the word "Sis" again.

Bengali courtesy taught me that the person who offered to buy a present usually insisted on buying it, and the person on the receiving end was to humbly decline. Nevertheless, after several "We insist" and "No, it's okay," the receiver surrenders. That was exactly what I did.

"Thank you, but I wouldn't know where to begin looking. All of the outfits are equally stunning."

"That's why I'm here, to guide you," Zamila stepped out from behind the counter and nudged me ahead.

"Yes, trust Zamila. She is the organizer of every fashion show at our school," Kushi said.

"You can trust Kushi too; she always helps me choose the outfits for the shows," Zamila said.

They led me to a counter, behind which *anarkalis* were. These were long A-line dresses with matching *ornas* or shawls. I let Zamila and Kushi choose my outfits for the trial room. Listening to their conversation and watching them reaching for fabrics and tossing them out in front of me, I couldn't help but laugh at times.

"How about this?" Zamila asked.

Kushi shut her eyes and answered for me, "Oh, that color is blinding me as much as the sun does when I look straight at it!"

"This one?" Kushi asked me.

Tongue-tied, I looked at the intricate embroidery and then up at Zamila, who said, "Too much going on; she

wants to look elegant, not *embellished* like a disco ball."
Zamila rummaged through some outfits and took one out
to show us.

"Isn't that what Americans wear to funerals?"
Kushi commented. "All black, not a hint of gold, silver, or
shimmer anywhere?!" I had already burst into laughter as
Zamila winced.

"Now, I am getting offended, Kushi!"

"Oh, you always get too serious when it comes to
fashion!" She put her arm around her best friend's
shoulders. "Zamila wants to be a designer some day!"

"That's wonderful," I said. "What do you want to
be, Kushi?"

Her smile had disappeared behind a mysterious
melancholy. *Why would such a simple question affect her
so...negatively? Don't they get asked this question here? Was it against
Bengali social decorum to ask about the future?*

70

Zamila immediately grew protective of Kushi, asking, "What are *your* dreams, Asha?" That's when I gathered it wasn't against Bengali social decorum to ask, after all. It was just a question my cousin seemed to dislike.

"I want to become an English professor."

"Impressive! You didn't even take a breath before answering."

"I guess it's easy when you know what you want to be. It's okay if you're still figuring that out," I addressed my cousin, who seemed to be lost in her own thoughts. She stared at the beige anarkali that Zamila had just draped over the counter. With net lining, lots of tulle and pearl embroidery, the dress seemed so...exquisite. *Perhaps Kushi was equally dumbfounded by its beauty? Perhaps I should just start getting used to her silence?*

"You must read a lot, then," Zamila said, her arms swallowing up the anarkali.

"I write, too."

"She has the most wonderful blog!" Kushi finally spoke.

"Oh?" Zamila signaled with her head to follow her, leaving Kushi alone. "What do you blog about?"

"Oh, anything...everything. It's like my journal except...."

"You lay your heart out for the world to see?" She interjected, hanging up the anarkali on a hook in the changing room.

"Well...yes, basically."

"Why?" She tilted her head, probing my eyes with her curious ones.

"Why, what?" We were surrounded by decadent wallpaper and standing on a luxurious Persian carpet.

"Why do you share your mind, heart and soul with the world? Isn't it too personal...too private?"

I chuckled. Zamila stared at me.

"It's funny because I've asked myself that question many times. But then, one day, I was walking in the rain and I answered that question *with* a question…. What's the point of having words if not to share them with someone, impact them in some way, however small or big?'"

"So…like, someone out there, who has nobody else to talk to, could possibly speak with you through your blog?" I suddenly wished that it were Kushi and I having this conversation, opening up to each other. The sad truth was that her having used the term "Sis" when addressing me seemed empty…lacking.

I nodded at Zamila. "Someone somewhere might need to read it and know that they're not alone."

"Let me know if you need any help; I'll be right outside," she said as she stepped out, allowing me to change into the anarkali.

Anarkalis are flowy and puffy. I put it on the floor and crawled into it from underneath. It felt like I was crawling through a narrow cave in search of light at the other end of it. I made it through that journey, suddenly remembering Mary Wollstonecraft Shelley and the challenge hoop skirts might have presented for her and other women during her time. Zamila zipped me up at the back. I turned around to look at my reflection in the oversized, intricately-sculpted, golden-rimmed mirror. Much to my surprise, I looked and felt as regal as that mirror was.

Zamila took two steps back, looked me up and down through her curly curls and made an *A-Okay* sign with her fingers.

Patting down the dress and swaying from side to side to see how it fit my body, I asked Zamila, "You don't think it's too much?"

"Oh, Sweetheart...." She touched my shoulders and put her chin on one of them. We looked into the same mirror as she continued, "Here, in Bangladesh, this is simply *elegance* and *you* are glowing in it."

"Thank you. You're so lucky! This shop is basically your walk-in closet. You can have your pick any day!"

"It has its perks." She unzipped me and left.

After changing back into my original white salwar kameez, I exited the changing room to see Zamila and Kushi looking at a maroon saree amidst a whole collection of sarees in varying shades of red, including burgundy, crimson, cherry, and mahogany. I joined them, the anarkali in hand. All that tulle and heavy embroidery weighed my arms down and strained my muscles.

"Are any of you getting married soon?" I asked.

"What?" Kushi asked in a defensive tone.

"Isn't red traditional for Bangladeshi brides?" I smiled because I wasn't serious when I asked, but it would soon become apparent that my cousin and her BFF were *taking* the question *seriously*.

Kushi opened her mouth to speak when Zamila beat her to it, "Times have changed. Red, although traditional, is no longer considered the *only* option for brides. Also, unmarried girls can wear red too."

I looked up and noticed posters of models posing as brides hanging above that particular counter. There was an image of a bride and a groom taking a stroll together, passing the columns of some grand palace. There was a photograph of a bride surrounded by her bridesmaids, who were helping her get ready for her big day. There was even a close-up image of a bride looking straight into the camera lens, her enigmatic eyes like those of the "Mona Lisa Effect," following our every move. Her lips were jungle red and her eyes outlined by a deep charcoal color and long, flirtatious eyelashes. Her gaze was intense, but I could not understand why: *Was it the seriousness of marriage? Was it the disappointment in her groom, soon-to-be husband? Had they gotten into a fight? Was it the fact that her life would change forever and she was unsure of how, exactly? Was it because of all of the above?* I felt my heart hopscotch a beat as I met that bride's exact same intense gaze in my cousin's eyes.

Kushi robotically said, "Zamila, show my cousin matching jewelry for her anarkali." Just like that, she momentarily subtracted me from her life, and I couldn't help but wonder what she was hiding. *Perhaps, I had been making things bigger than they actually were? Perhaps, Kushi wasn't hiding anything of any significance at all?* Yet, my intuitions fought against those doubts as Zamila practically dragged

77

me to the jewelry counter. She took out a set of pearl chandelier earrings with matching *tikli*, a traditional Bangladeshi headpiece.

"I know what you're doing." I was referring to the fact that Kushi had telepathically asked Zamila to distract me while she looked at bridal clothes and jewelry.

Zamila robotically replied, "Asha, I'm showing you our jewelry collection and I think this one would best match your outfit. We have similar designs, though. Take your pick." She tapped her finger on the glass encasement as if to say, *keep your eyes here and only here*. Throughout this entire situation, I suddenly realized that I wasn't speaking to some random girl I had just met in Bangladesh; rather, I was speaking to someone who had known Kushi much better than I had...who was more of a sister to her than I was. Zamila was my key to understanding Kushi.

I clucked my tongue against my teeth. "I like the one you picked." As she wrapped the tikli up and placed it in a box, I whispered to her, "Zamila, last night, Kushi's phone vibrated and she suddenly got tense and nervous. And then, there was a motorcycle sound outside of the house and she was so scared…."

"So, you know about him?" She looked up at me, perplexed and concerned.

"Yes, I know…about *him*," I lied while attempting to hide my surprise.

"Then, I guess she told you about her crazy plan, eh?"

Quick, think of something….

"Zamila!" Kushi called her over before I could brainstorm an answer.

Kushi and a "him?" Crazy plan? Bridal sarees! Was Kushi going to elope with a guy?!

"Could you put these on layaway?" Kushi asked Zamila. She nodded in agreement.

My head reeled with the assumption...Kushi and a secret fiancé zooming off on the back of *his* motorcycle in the middle of the night, only to return home the next morning as a married woman! *No, no, this cannot be. Stop making assumptions before you get the facts!*

Kushi purchased my anarkali and matching jewelry for me. Zamila followed us out for her lunch break. She handed me the plastic shopping bag, which had a beautiful bridal image printed on it. I thanked Zamila and hugged Kushi.

"Thank you so much for this dress and jewelry. You *really* didn't have to, you know?"

She held my hand again, although this time...not as firmly as when we had first arrived at the shopping district.

"Of course, we had to, Sis. It's your first time shopping with me. I would never have let you go without a gift."

Despite the fact that we were holding hands, the word "Sis" seemed as far out of my reach as the galaxies. Meanwhile, I imagined the worst scenarios of this bride-to-be...at *my* age. A 17-year-old bride just didn't sit right with me.

We ordered some Thai soup and noodles. As we sat there, waiting for our orders, Zamila talked about the last fashion show she had organized at their school.

"And then, Jenny got what was coming to her. I warned her about the size of those heels! It wasn't my fault she stumbled, fell and sprained her ankle! Her parents tried to sue me!"

"So, the stereotype fits!" I said.

They both stared at me.

"Models are such divas!"

We laughed until, out of nowhere, a low rumbling of a motorcycle screeched its way toward the entrance of the restaurant. All of us grew quiet, held our breaths in, and sat still, speaking to one another only with our eyes; I sensed my cousin's fear, the smell of it was pungent, the look of it was paralyzing. Still, we refused to realize the fact that even if we did not move an inch, even if we did not inhale and exhale loudly...we would still be anything *but* invisible. Who could have ignored my cousin's beauty? Like a siren, she had summoned a man to our table.

He looked only at her as he strolled in, put his hand on Zamila's shoulder to nudge her aside and sat down in her place, right next to Kushi. His right shoulder brushed against Kushi's left one. Still statuesque, my cousin kept her eyes on me as if pleading for *help*. Who was this man, his hair as dark and sublime as his stoic facial expression and unreadable eyes? Who was this man in a leather jacket that smelled like it had only just been purchased; each of his knuckles caressing crisply-outlined rings, his lips full of lust, rested above the shadow of a beard? Could this be the "him" that Zamila had divulged to me earlier at her parents' shop? If this was "him," her potential *fiance*, why wasn't my cousin more excited to see him?

The man then turned to me, and stuck his hand out, revealing a row of scars along his wrist. "Hi, I'm Josh Costa." I couldn't help but giggle a little when he said his name as I shook his hand.

"I'm sorry for laughing. I just never met a Bangladeshi with a name like that before! Nice to meet you."

He smirked.

"Anyway, I'm...." I began.

"Asha, I know. Kushi told me you were coming. From America, right?"

"Yes, New York City. Sorry, but I haven't heard *anything* about you," I nonchalantly said.

He narrowed his eyes at Kushi as if she had done something wrong. She said, "Of course, I told you about Josh, but you were probably jetlagged and too busy unpacking to notice."

Unpacking? Abdul and Zulekha did the unpacking for me! Noticing Kushi's eyes begging me to lie, I did just that.

"Now that I think of it," I said, "You did mention a guy!" I feigned a smile at Josh.

"Well...I hope I'm the *only* guy," he said.

Just then, I understood that my speaking only made my cousin's hands quiver. It also made Zamila glare at me because she realized that I had lied to her about knowing anything about a "him" in my cousin's life.

Josh put his hands on my cousin's and whispered into her ear, although loud enough for us to hear, "I know

I'm *the only one.*" He fingered a few of her hair strands. His cologne surrounded us like fog, thickening more and more with his every move. It seeped its way into my throat, folded into layers and stayed there until he got up and started to leave.

"Josh, can I get you anything?" The waiter asked.

"No, but thank you for asking, Kholiq."

"Anytime, Josh. Give my regards to your parents."

"And mine to yours."

With that, the waiter walked off.

He took a sip of Kushi's soda, got up and began walking away again. Just as my cousin seemed to breathe a little easier, we heard him ask, "Aren't you coming, Kushi, my *jaan*? "Jaan" is Bengali for "life," which is used to address the love of one's life.

85

Kushi got up cautiously and followed Josh as solemnly as a funeral procession. As soon as they left the restaurant, Zamila confronted me.

"You said you knew about *him*!"

"Okay, I lied! But it's only because I'm worried about my cousin, whom I only just met yesterday and she's having trouble opening up to me. You and I, we don't know each other that well, Zamila, but in the short time we spoke at your parents' shop, I feel like I know *you* better than I know my own cousin...and that's not okay, is it?"

Zamila grabbed my arm and pulled me toward the restaurant window that looked out onto the street. She and I watched Josh, sitting on his motorcycle, helmet in hand, angrily lecturing Kushi about something.

"Zamila," I whispered.

"Huh?"

"We are 17 years old."

She kept looking outside of the window.

"Don't you have to be over 18 years old to drive a motorcycle?"

"That's correct," she replied.

"How old is Josh, exactly?"

"24." The number rolled off her tongue and landed at my feet. I picked it up and threw it back at her.

"24?!"

Zamila clasped my mouth with her hand and shushed me.

"Josh is 24 years old and Kushi is 17 years old," I thought out loud.

Zamila shrugged her shoulders like it was the most normal relationship to have. Back in America, this would have been considered a crime; Kushi was a minor and Josh might as well be labeled a pedophile... handcuffed, and tossed into a jail cell!

"She was looking at bridal sarees today. Are they...are they getting married?" I gulped hard at the thought.

"No! Of course, not! But she's not telling *Josh* that. She's just going to let him think whatever he wants to think."

"So, she's playing pretend, which is good news?"

Zamila rolled her eyes at me.

"I'm confused, though. If Kushi's not getting married to him, then why was she looking at bridal sarees?" Zamila was about to answer when I interrupted, "And do not tell me about how you don't need to be a bride to wear red because although that might be true, I'm not stupid enough to believe *that* is the case *here*!"

"Frankly speaking," Zamila began, "I don't think I am the right person to be answering your questions."

88

She was right. I had to ask Kushi. I had to give her the chance to let me in.

Just then, we saw Kushi attempting to walk back into the restaurant when Josh grabbed her orna, which was wrapped around her neck. He then pulled her back toward him like he was a cowboy at a rodeo who had just caught his prized bull.

Josh twisted the orna tighter and tighter around her neck until she gagged. I got up, ready to run outside and rescue her, but Zamila grabbed my arm and pulled me so hard that I slipped and fell onto the floor, landing right on my coccyx.

"You can't go out there! Trust me, it'll make things worse for her," she pleaded.

"What?! This is crazy!" My eyes frantically searched for answers in the atoms and molecules. I felt trickles of sweat sliding down from my forehead to my lips. I could taste the saltiness as much as the bitterness of what was happening to my cousin.

"Trust me. As much as he hurts her, he won't kill her," Zamila said as if the words "hurt" and "kill" were napkins I could use to pat my sweat away with. I watched Zamila turn away from the scene and walk back to our table. She sat down and slurped up the cold soup, pretending like nothing was happening to her best friend. She seemed just as desensitized to it as the passers-by on the streets were. But...she was my cousin's best friend! I felt wrath crawling its way up from my guts to my esophagus until all I wanted to do was roar at the top of my lungs at this dumb, stupid girl whom my cousin dubbed her "BFF." Most of all, I wanted to get rid of this monstrosity of a man who had been haunting my cousin, creeping and crawling up outside of her window in the middle of the night.

I took out my phone and started filming what was happening. If I wasn't allowed to go outside to save my cousin, I thought that the least I could do was record proof in case it could save her in the future. I had a feeling that one day...some day, we would need these videos. *Videos* and not *video* because I sensed it wasn't going to be the first time we'd encounter Josh Costa during my stay. After all, it certainly wasn't Kushi's first time, nor Zamila's. His eyes were wide, the red veins forming rivers around his pupils, visible even from a distance. He looked outraged but showed Kushi some mercy.

As soon as he released her from his grasp, Kushi coughed as she made her way back toward the restaurant entrance. She did not enter, though. Instead, she waited until Josh *zoomed* away on his motorcycle. She then took out her phone, put it in selfie mode and faked a smile that might have convinced the world she was okay and happy. Deep down, I knew she wasn't and I refused to believe that Josh Costa was anything close to the man of her dreams. One thing was for certain, Kushi didn't need to convince me of her beauty. What she really needed to do was to convince herself of that, to truly see how worthy she was of every dream she could possibly imagine to achieve. Josh was not it; in fact, he did not deserve to even step foot in her shadow.

With that thought, I watched Kushi walk back inside. She noticed me standing close to the window and most likely guessed that I had been spying on her and Josh. I smiled as warmly as I could at her; I hoped my smile held her in its arms, consoled her, let her know that everything was going to be okay from now on because she had a *real*

BFF here instead of the fake one, carelessly sipping away at her soup. She frowned and without a word, walked back to our table. She didn't seem to have much of an appetite left and I wondered if that was the secret to how slender she was; if *fear* was her secret diet. If so, that was a diet I would never want to try nor recommend to anyone. The silence was back; it had creeped up on us just as subtly and slyly as Josh Costa had. And yet, I tried to make conversation as a distraction.

"Um, so...the chaatpoti stand was awesome!"

Kushi said nothing. She just kept looking down at her hands.

"Oh, I love that food stand! Although it does give me stomach cramps, all that spice," Zamila said. I was mad at her for not understanding what I was trying to do. I grew more and more enraged with every word she uttered. "Did you try their *fushka?*" She asked.

93

"Their what?" I asked through clenched teeth.

Maybe if we keep talking, Kushi will join in.

"Fushka is the little crunchy fried dough that puffs up like a balloon and then you pop a hole in the center of it to fill the inside with chaatpoti and tamarind sauce."

"Ah...right," I said, having no idea what she was talking about. "We have to try that one day, Kushi!"

She nodded, her eyes fixated on her hands as if they were cuffed or chained.

Zamila finally owned up to her title of "BFF" and said, "Kushi, you know I'm here for you if you need to talk about...anything, you know, whatever." Upon noticing her genuine eyes peep through her curly curls, I questioned whether or not I had been too quick and harsh to judge her role in Kushi's life.

"I know," Kushi replied with a grin.

It was good hearing her voice again and seeing somewhat of a smile on her face, but I couldn't help but feel slightly envious of Zamila. The whole time I had been secretly criticizing her for being a bad BFF, while I, myself, didn't show her any concern about what had *actually* happened. Instead, I talked about food stands.... *Way to go, Asha! You've certainly proved yourself worthy of being BFF, let alone earning the title of "Sis." NOT.*

As they continued their silent conversation through their eyes, sighs, grins and nods, I took out *Frankenstein,* the only friend I had at the moment or rather, the only friend I thought I deserved: *"The sun rose; I heard the voices of men and knew that it was impossible to return to my retreat during that day. Accordingly I hid myself in some thick underwood, determining to devote the ensuing hours to reflection on my situation."* "We need light for example, sunlight, to awaken our thoughts," I

95

whispered what I had written next to the quote. I then looked up to see if anyone had heard me. They hadn't...so I devoted *the ensuing hours to reflection on my situation.* Actually, I just kept reading my pencil-marked notes in *Frankenstein* until my cousin and Zamila were ready to leave.

CHAPTER 4

THE RED SUN

It wasn't a myth, after all. The Bangladeshi rising

sun was, indeed, *red*. Its flames wavered just as the red circle

did at the center of the Bangladeshi flag. The shades of red,

including ruby, crimson and mahogany, were just as enticing

as the varying shades of bridal sarees Kushi had rummaged

through the day before. I was suddenly reminded of my

cousin's melancholic boy trouble, to put it lightly. As

uninspiring as it was, a side to Bangladesh I didn't want to

see, I closed my eyes in an attempt to replace that memory

with something more pleasant. I felt the warmth of the sun like a quilt over my eyelids and I knew that this was the opportunity to get better acquainted with Bangladesh.

I had performed *namaz* or *salah*, my morning Islamic prayer and sat on the rooftop of Kushi's house. The rooftop was surrounded by rows of flowers in pots, including marigolds, jasmines and roses. There were a couple of plastic chairs and a round table. A rope ran from one end of the rooftop to the other end, where I assumed Zulekha hung up our washed clothes to dry. Abdul had just brought me some warm chai, the smell of cardamoms and cinnamon kissed my nose. I took a sip from the small, pristinely white teacup. I then picked up my pen and began writing in My Little Tanzanite for the next blog entry. I would highlight the positive things about the day before: how I went shopping with my cousin and met her best friend and how my cousin, aunt and uncle, had gifted me with a gorgeous anarkali and matching jewelry. I would post photographs of the multicolored sandals aligning the wall of one shop, of my anarkali, of the poor children chasing cars, and of the busy streets filled with vibrant rickshaws, CNG's, buses, cars, trucks and...*motorcycles*. I grimaced upon thinking the last word and wondered if I should be completely ignoring Kushi's boy trouble...if ignoring it was even the correct way to handle it. *Why did such a cool vehicle have to be associated with being badass in its most negative connotation?*

"Good morning, Sis."

I looked up, squinting one eye. "Kushi? Good morning!" I immediately put my pen down and closed my journal. She was speaking to me! And she called me, "Sis."

"What are you doing up here?" She asked. She had on a pink salwar kameez that brought out the rosiness of her cheeks. I was still in my polka-dotted kaftan.

"Getting inspired," I answered, tapping my closed journal with my pen.

"On the rooftop? There's not much of a view from up here, just...other rooftops."

"No, there's much more to see." I pointed to the sky.

Kushi looked up, one hand above her eyebrows to shade her from the sunlight.

There were some black drongos flying around. She took a deep breath and sat down in the chair across the table from me.

"Oh, Asha, doesn't the whole world share the same sky?" Her giggles chimed toward me, hugging me, like the sound of *nupors* hugging the ankles of a traditional Bengali dancer.

"Believe it or not, the sky is a lot less visible where I live in America....What are *you* doing up here?" I asked.

"Looking for you, actually. Abdul told me you were here, so...I wanted to talk."

"Sure, let's talk!" I tried not to sound too eager but obviously failed.

Should I mention anything about what happened yesterday? Asha, don't pressure her!

She and I had ridden the CNG back, in silence, for the most part, Kushi looking down at her hands and I, looking down at *Frankenstein*. On our way from the shopping district, the poor kids chased us, yelling, "Londoni Madam!" We managed to hand out some cash before we ran out. Kushi had to yell a number of times, "We don't have anymore!" Meanwhile, I wondered why these kids kept calling us "Londoni" and not "American." Was "American" too difficult of a word for them to pronounce or did UK Bengali residents visit Bangladesh a lot more often than American Bengali residents did? Or did the kids just randomly use the words "Londoni" one day and "American" the next? As soon as we got back and stepped out of the vehicle, Kushi insisted again on paying the driver before stomping into the house, only to avoid me the rest of the day.

Instead of asking myself what it was that *I* had done wrong, I made peace with the idea that, perhaps, my cousin just needed space. On the rooftop, Abdul came up with a cup of chai for Kushi. She thanked him as he left.

"Nice," she said, pointing to her nose.

"Huh?" Was this some sort of Bengali custom I wasn't aware of? *Should I also point to my nose?*

"That nose ring looks good on you," she said, pointing at the stud on my nose. "It's cool that you chose a sapphire stud."

"Oh! Thank you. When we got home last night, Amma took me out again to get my nose pierced. Blue's my favorite color, so a sapphire seemed appropriate. I almost forgot I had it!"

"It will take some time getting used to." She took a sip of her chai. "Did it hurt?"

"Not as much as I thought it would. I still held Amma's hand, though, just in case."

"Aw, that's so cute! I love the relationship you two have, kind of like...friends."

I nodded. "Don't you and your mom have the same? Khala seems chill."

"Chill...." She repeated before she laughed.

As much as I enjoyed our little chit-chat, I wondered out loud, "So...was there anything specific you wanted to talk about? Anything you want to share with me?"

"It's about what happened yesterday with...Josh." She picked up the teacup with shaky hands and drank from it. As she placed the cup back on the saucer, I heard it rattle.

"Um, it's complicated. I'm not sure how to explain it without it taking me hours out of your day...."

"I'm on vacation, Kushi. I am in no hurry and you can take your time, okay?" I put my hand on hers, hoping it would comfort her.

"I might cry," she warned.

"And if you do, is it okay if I hold you?" *Because ultimately, that's what sisters are for, or so I've heard.*

She nodded, her eyes already glazed. She looked up toward the sky, inhaled deeply the red sun's rays and released it toward me. "I was on my way home from school two months ago. A group of gang members on motorcycles surrounded me. One of them took off my orna, another pulled my bag away from me and a third grabbed hold of my arm and tried to get me to sit on the back of his bike." Her hands began to shake, so I held them and tried to meet her eyes.

"It's okay, Kushi. You're fine," *because that day is in the past.* Little did I understand *then*, that things from the past were not always meant to stay there.

She sniffed up and gulped down tears, struggling to continue.

She managed to say, "I couldn't decide whether to fight back or to give in. The scariest part, Asha, was that I was so close to home, but nobody could hear my screams over the noise of their motorcycles...except one, Josh Costa.

He came in on his bike, grabbed my bag and orna from the gang members, grabbed me by my waist, swooped me up onto the back of his bike and sped off.

The others didn't follow. Still, I wondered if he was one of them, you know? If what had happened was all part of some grand plan that they had mustered up together. Sometimes, I still wonder if he is one of them..."

"After what happened yesterday, I can understand

that." Then, I realized that yesterday was just one day of many days for my cousin-two months, to be exact!

"As he drove off with me, he said, 'I'll take you home. Where do you live?' Reluctantly, I told him my address and... he dropped me off at our gate. Then, he sped off before I could thank him."

"Heroic! Chivalrous! Knight in shining armor!" Sarcasm punched me in the face.

Kushi snorted. "Yeah.... Actually, he was a perfect gentleman...*at first*...until his true colors finally revealed themselves. I didn't want to tell Amma and Abba about what had happened because I didn't want to worry them; I just kept it a secret no matter how much it ate me up inside. To this day, they know nothing and I prefer it that way. Since the day I met Josh, I despised the sound of motorcycles. When I do hear it, my stomach feels like it's about to crawl up my throat to the point where I could vomit it out and my head feels like it could boulder off my neck, down my shoulders and into a gutter somewhere. Yet, one day, I heard it outside of my home again. It had only been a couple of days since the incident. Josh Costa showed up outside of our house gate. As soon as I stepped outside, I recognized his motorcycle and leather jacket. He seemed to be waiting for me. He noticed I was in my school uniform, the same old white and light blue, and offered me a ride to school. I was hesitant at first. After all, he was a complete stranger. I had yet to know his name.

"'I'm Josh, Josh Costa. What's your name?' he asked.

"As soon as I said my name, he just swooped me up onto the back of his motorcycle again and drove off. 'What's the address to your school?' He asked me. And…he dropped me off at school."

We both took a sip of our chai.

I asked, "So, that's how it all began? You basically just gave him your home address and your school address. Stalker much?"

Kushi replied, "Yes and unfortunately, it hasn't stopped since and I'm not sure if it ever will. He takes me to school every day. During our rides together, we talk."

"About...?"

"Everything...anything. He told me things like how his mother owns a famous fashion design house in Dhaka. How his father owns a successful furniture shop in Sylhet and is well-connected and highly-respected, even by the police and some government officials, that even my father might know his name. Of course, I never asked Abba. Josh also told me about his pet dog and how close they are, but how vicious and untrained it is. I told him about my parents too, my cousin in America...." She smiled at me. "And how I hate math, that my favorite color is turquoise and I love reading books in the English language. And then, one day…." She gulped down more tears, but some drops escaped. My cousin began sobbing.

"Hey, it's okay." But it wasn't okay and I felt stupid for my poor choice of words. "Take your time." *Better choice of words!*

Kushi took another sip of her chai only to realize there was none left to quench her thirst on. I offered her my cup, which she accepted. She took a sip and wiped away her tears with her fingertips.

"One day…." She cleared her throat. "One day, I was coming out of school, talking to Zamila and another classmate whom we call, Jug. I bid them 'Goodbye' as I got onto the back of Josh's motorcycle. He was quiet, which seemed…uncanny. I asked him what was wrong…why was he so quiet. He asked, 'Who was that guy with you today?' I replied, 'Just a classmate.' 'Do you walk that closely with all of your guy classmates?' He asked. I didn't know how to respond. 'Well, do you?!" He yelled, startling me. When I didn't speak, he abruptly stopped the motorcycle and I fell to the ground, scraping my leg. Bleeding and whimpering, I sat down on the ground, waiting for him to reach out his hand to help me up, to save me just as he did on that day...from the gang members." She stopped to wipe away more tears.

"He just watched me suffer and then rode off. I thought I would never see him again, which at that point, would have been totally fine with me...but the next day, there he was again, waiting for me outside of the house gate. I was so mad at him that I ignored him and started walking away. He ran after me, grabbed my arm, twirled me around, led me into an alleyway. I could hear a cat shriek as I almost stepped on it. And I thought he was going to...you know...."

I assumed she meant that he was going to rape her, but I refused to utter the word out loud.

"He grabbed me by the waist, pushed his chest really hard against my breasts." She seemed to be hyperventilating.

All I could think of doing was rub her back as she continued, "I gasped for air, but I couldn't breathe...I couldn't breathe, but he *was* breathing. He was breathing really hard. And then...he pushed his lips against mine." Kushi was looking down at her other empty teacup. I just stared at her, wondering if there was more to it while hoping that there wasn't.

"You didn't want him to...*did* you?" I asked hesitantly, partly because I wasn't sure exactly where Kushi drew the line with Josh.

"Of course, I didn't want him...at all! I don't want him. I was so scared, Asha. I wasn't sure where that kiss would lead. I know I should be grateful that's all that happened, but still...I felt so naked; I felt...."

"Violated? Harassed? Sexually assaulted by a pedophile?" *Try not to sound so direct and insensitive, Asha!*

She nodded as she sobbed. "After that, he didn't release me. He clasped his hand on my mouth, pushing the back of my head more against the wall and whispered a warning into my ear."

I imagined him doing this, the hair strands of my cousin scraping against the wall of some building in an alleyway, etching into it a cry for help with nobody present to hear it... *I wasn't there.* Being there now, though, I kept rubbing her back as she tried to breathe with more ease. I was eager to know what he had whispered into her ear, but I waited patiently for Kushi to speak.

"He said, 'You're mine. Next time you resist me, ignore me, offend me in any way, you will become *completely* untouchable.' He sounded like he was growling under his breath. He left me there, alone. I heard him ride off on his motorcycle. Shaking, I stood there, questioning whether or not I should go to school. I was afraid that my teachers and classmates could see through me, fear and shock written all over my face. So, I went back inside the house, told Amma and Abba that I was feeling sick and I crawled back under the covers, only to replay what had happened over and over again in my head." She folded her arms, rubbing them up and down as if she felt a chill.

I imagined my cousin, under her covers, sinking deeper and deeper beneath it and drowning herself in her tears...kind of like what she was doing just then. The top part of her orna was completely drenched.

"I'm just so ashamed of myself for letting a man like Josh into my life."

I forced her to meet my eyes. "He forced his way into your life and *he's* the one that should be ashamed for what he's doing to you!" In the most delicate manner I could, I said, "Kushi, let's stop that son-of-a-...."

"*We* can't. You cannot get involved. He's *dangerous*." She whispered the last word as if it were some fatal secret. As if just uttering the word could kill us.

Two months and ongoing stalked and harassed by a 24-year-old pedophile, my cousin needed to escape his wrath and I was going to help her do it!

I took out my phone and showed Kushi the video I had recorded the day before, where he nearly choked her outside of the restaurant.

As soon as the video stopped playing, I noticed her frowning.

"What's wrong? We have proof! You should be ecstatic!"

"It's just...I look so pathetic. I look so weak. I'm ashamed of myself for being that way with him. It's...embarrassing!" She shook her head.

"You need to stop identifying yourself with the words 'ashamed' and 'embarrassed.' Get those words out of your head! You are the strongest person I know, carrying this burden around, all by yourself, simply to protect everyone around you from...*him*. You're not alone. You have me, Zamila...your parents."

"Never!" Kushi screamed as she stood up from the plastic chair so abruptly that it flew backward and fell with a thump to the ground. "My parents can never know! Neither can yours! They would go to the police and that won't help because Josh's family has deep ties with the police department. They would want to attack him, but they wouldn't be able to because Josh has his own gang hidden away somewhere; he has a ruthless and dangerous dog that could tear them apart. He's capable of so much and I'm not...I'm not his first."

"What do you mean?"

"There were other girls."

"Were?" I did not want to imagine what had happened to them. "There were other victims?"

"Victims?" She repeated the word like it was the first time anyone had called her that, like it was the first time she realized she *was* that, a *victim*. "He's never told me about the other...victims, but I hear things, things he's done, things that no girl my age or younger should experience. So...I try to be obedient."

I stood up, picked up the chair and sat her back down. I kneeled down in front of her, pressed my palm tightly against hers. "I'm here for you. I want to help, but I need to know *everything*...tell me everything you know about Josh and what he's done to you."

"You can't know." She vigorously shook her head.

"How dangerous is he, Kushi? Tell me, or I'll tell my mom." I hated using blackmail as a tactic, but it was all I had left. I was desperate. The imaginary door was ajar but not wide enough to fully let me in. *Let me in, Kushi!*

"At first," she began, "I thought he was just being nice, but then, it was like my slightest move made him angry. He just wanted me to be like a doll, still until *he* moved me. When my classmates noticed him dropping me off at school and picking me up from school every day, they started spreading rumors about us. I thought they had no idea how much of a control he had over me, that they couldn't possibly understand the real story...until Zamila told me that I wasn't his first. She told me that he's well-known for exploiting young girls such as myself. That was when I realized my classmates knew what was going on, but they felt helpless; all they felt they could do was watch. One day, he and I were near a lake; he rolled up his sleeves to wash his face and I noticed some scars on his wrist. When I asked him about them, he told me that he had carved them into his skin with a knife. He said there was something about blood and healing that created a bodily connection to the people he loved. Each scar represented someone special in his life. And then...he showed me the scar he made to 'honor' me. I already felt like a distant memory to him, like someone he could make disappear if he wanted to. Asha, there were too many scars for me to count; they were overlapping. And that scares the life out of me."

To *honor* her? Kushi had been reduced to trickles of blood, to the crackling of a scab and then to an accumulation of skin layers that covered each other up until healed, yet visible of what it once was, pain. *Too many scars to count; they were overlapping?* She was right...Josh could make her disappear if he wanted to. I looked at this girl whose

118

body was curled up, swaying back and forth, burying her face into her orna, trying to stop herself from shivering, from sobbing. She had warned me this would happen, so I did exactly as I had promised her...I hugged her, saying, "It's okay, Sis." Suddenly, I felt a warmth swarming around us; the red sun held us in its arms, rocked us back and forth and whispered into our ears, "Everything is going to be okay." I wondered if Kushi had heard it too.

"Kushi!" A harsh voice shattered the moment. It was that of my aunt, Kushi's mother. "Kushi!" Khala sounded so angry.

Kushi quickly ran down the stairs from the rooftop, into the bathroom to wash her face and fake a smile.

I waited for her and held her hand as we ran down the stairs into the living room.

"Salam!" I greeted Khala.

"Oh, Asha, *walaikum assalam*. You're up early!"

"Yes. And so are you."

An awkward silence lingered above us, ready to swoop down and engulf us before....

"I was hoping I could speak to Kushi alone if you don't mind."

"Okay, I'll just...." I began before Kushi interrupted.

"I don't mind if Asha is here."

My aunt handed Kushi a letter.

She opened it up. It was written in Bengali and I wasn't that great at reading my mother tongue. My parents attempted to teach me how to read and write in the Bengali language growing up and it became difficult to maintain that knowledge every time school reopened after the summer break.

All I could read at that moment was my cousin's facial expression. It looked grim.

"This isn't what you think, Amma. It must be some kind of a joke."

"Who's Josh?"

My eyes widened and then, I tried to hide my shock by looking away, anywhere else but at the letter or at my aunt. I failed.

"Asha, is there something you know about my daughter that you're not telling me?"

I solemnly shook my head, hoping she would buy it.

"Amma, this is a prank. All the girls in my class are getting these in their mail. Even Zamila," Kushi lied and she did it surprisingly well.

I was close enough to my mother to tell her things, but I guessed Kushi and her mother were not *that* close. Why was she lying to her? Why couldn't she just tell her the truth? How much longer was she going to think that keeping this secret about Josh was going to protect her parents? These thoughts weighed me down like an anchor set loose, sinking deeper and deeper into the shallow.

"Breakfast is ready," Zulekha interrupted.

Khala said nothing.

Kushi said nothing.

I ... said nothing.

But then someone said something. "Oh, Joyti, you are up so early these days! I hope we're not too much trouble for you," Abba said, descending the staircase.

Kushi hid the letter behind her back and smiled at him.

Khala feigned a smile as well. "Not at all, *Bhai*. Come, come, breakfast is on the table." The word "Bhai" means "brother" in the Bengali language. In-laws were really considered that much like family in the Bengali culture!

As the two of them settled down at the table, Kushi and I snuck back upstairs. We ran into Amma and Khalu on the way up.

"Where are you girls off to?"

"Forgot something. We'll be down soon!" I yelled as we went back to the rooftop. It seemed to be the safest of headquarters for us, girls, minus the batmobile and costumes. Kushi read the letter to me:

Dear Parents of Kushi, I am in love with your daughter and I know she loves me, too. I ask you for her hand in marriage. If you should consent, I will inform my parents and we can come over. Sincerely, Josh Costa, Son of Raj Costa and Tanshara Costa.

"So, that's what he meant…." Kushi looked up at me as if the red sun's solar energy lit her up.

"What?"

"Yesterday, he confronted me about something that I couldn't understand until now. He thought I had

123

rejected his marriage proposal. But, I hadn't even seen his letter until now."

So, that's why he tortured and humiliated my cousin outside, in broad daylight, in public!

"How many days did he give you to accept his marriage offer, Kushi?" I asked, assuming there was some sort of ultimatum that bought us time.

"Two weeks…. And that's him being generous."

"Generous" was used to describe a person whose heart was larger and fuller than necessary. That attribute was often used as a compliment and it certainly did *not* apply to Josh Costa.

I grabbed the letter from Kushi's hands and tossed it aside. I grabbed her by the shoulders and looked at her in the eyes. "You," I concluded, "are going to survive the wrath of Josh Costa. I will make sure of it."

Kushi released her gaze from my eyes, shrugged her shoulders so that I could release them and turned away from me. "You cannot get involved in this. I won't let you submerge yourself in the same fear that I am drowning in."

"I live and breathe fear, Kushi!"

"Oh, you mean in your books? I saw you reading 'Frankenstein' yesterday. You don't live and breathe fear like I do; fear, for you, is when you open that book and it ends as soon as you close it. I can't do that! My life is non-fiction!"

"But…I want to help…."

"I know…I know." I looked down at my sandals until I noticed Kushi's pair was so close to mine that they almost touched.

When I looked up at her, she proclaimed, "I will survive. Don't worry. I have a plan which will be set in motion tomorrow."

"What kind of a plan?" I asked.

"It involves something that you, my dear sister, will gravely disapprove of."

"How do you know that?"

"In this little time that we've gotten to know one another, I understand that much."

"Kushi, how *stupid* is your plan?" I crossed my arms, guarding myself from what I was about to hear.

She laughed as she walked closer to the edge of the rooftop.

"Kushi? How *idiotic* is your plan?" At that point, I was getting mad at her, fearing the worst.

"Those are such harsh words, Asha." She smirked.

"I hear sibling rivalry is normal." And I had a feeling it was going to be brutal. I could have threatened to tell Khala and Khalu *everything*, but the truth was that it would have been just as empty a threat as most of the neighboring rooftops had been, barren and in need of marigolds, jasmines and roses. "I guess we won't be rubbing coconut oil into each other's scalps anytime soon."

As she stood close to the edge, I prayed she wouldn't do what I was thinking she was about to do. I stood close enough to hold her back in case she slipped. However, Kushi turned back around to look at me. As she moved toward me and away from the edge, I realized that she wasn't going to jump after all. I sighed with relief.

"Asha, sometimes it's okay...it's actually best for you...*not* to know everything, *not* to have to understand *everything.*

Was that a failed attempt at calming me down? I thought to myself. She might have thought it best for me not to know and understand everything, but what she hadn't realized was that I *needed* to know and understand everything. As I stood there, thinking just *that*, I watched my cousin, the girl who had called me "Sis," slip away from me just as quickly as sand particles seep through one's fingers. I had lost her trust just as quickly as I had gained it. However, I was determined to gain it back just as quickly as I had lost it.

CHAPTER 5

THE PROPOSAL

If it rained on a wedding day, apparently, it was meant to be "good luck." If the sun shined on a wedding day, apparently, it was meant to be "good luck." The purpose of saying these things, I guessed, was to calm the nerves, those same nerves that could grab someone by the head and shake it into extreme anxiety, sadness, outrage, or all three simultaneously.

Weddings, *ahem, Bengali* weddings, to sum it up, were anything but *calm*. There was nothing calm about hundreds of people packed into one room, observing a couple on stage, spotlights cooking the bride's heavily-embroidered orna on her head and the groom's thickly-turbaned head.

There was nothing calm about ravenous people following a disorganized assembly line to get their meals. If meals were served at the table, there was nothing calm about the types of conversations people exchanged.

"Ouch," I yelped.

The lady at the salon nearly poked me in the eye with her finger as she glued on my extra lashes. Kushi and I were getting dolled up at the local beauty parlor for the wedding we had been invited to. The makeup artist powdered my face a shade, maybe two, lighter than my actual skin tone. But, her eye-makeup techniques were superb. I had never seen my eyebrows and eyes look so striking before! We told the hairstylist we wanted to leave our hair in loose curls. When back at the house, I changed into the beige and pearl-embroidered anarkali my aunt and cousin had gifted me with. Kushi wore a similar design but in mint green. I was happy that I wasn't the only one looking like a chandelier, high up, at the center of the room. "Simple elegance" were the exact words Zamila had used to describe such clothes to me when I visited her parents' shop. Although I felt "elegant," I did not feel "simple."

"Is Zamila going to be at the wedding?" I asked Kushi while grabbing my clutch from the dressing table as we walked out of my bedroom. She had come in to check if I needed help with anything.

She looked gobsmacked. "Sorry, it's just that...you look stunning."

"Look who's talking! Thank you. So, will she be there?"

"No. Zamila and her family are not that closely acquainted with the bride or groom."

131

Kushi's eyes were shimmery, like mine. If there were a day people could easily mistake us for *real* sisters, this would be that day. If there were a day she could call me "Sis" without meaning it and still get away with it, *this* would be that day!

When we arrived at the wedding destination in the evening, I wondered if there was no sunshine or rain, then would the day be considered an auspicious day? We walked through a tunnel made of fresh, pink-and-white rose garlands, each rose strung together and wrapped around the skeleton of a tunnel. Some garlands dangled down from above as if it were raining roses. With that observation, I suddenly missed the rain.

"Does it ever rain during this time of year?" I asked Kushi.

"Yes, it does," Kushi answered. "Why?"

"I hope it does at some point."

"Aren't you here to escape the dreary, cold American air at this time of year?"

"That's just the thing about rain, Kushi; it doesn't have to be cold. It just fills me up with an unexplainable warmth."

She giggled. "Doesn't the red sun give you enough of that around here?!"

I laughed, knowing she wasn't entirely wrong. The sun was certainly my journal's best friend. Every time the red sun rose or set, its rays filled me up with words, lots and lots of words.

Some motorcycles *vroomed* past us and with every rumble, Kushi tightened her grip around my arm.

I was suddenly reminded of our small rivalry.

I needed to know and understand *everything*, but she wouldn't let me in. *Perhaps, the wedding event would give us the opportunity to build trust between us.*

We entered the wedding venue, where the chills of my thoughts were melted by a different kind of rain. We were showered by rose petals. As if the venue's luscious gold, copper and high ceilings weren't extravagant enough, sheets of white chiffons formed a canopy beneath them. There were tall bouquets in golden vases as centerpieces. The tablecloths were also pink and white, surrounded by plush, white velvet chairs that were outlined by gold metal. I finally felt like I fit in with my outfit; all of the guests looked like they were celebrities walking down a red carpet. I noticed the stage where the bride and groom sat.

"So, it's true," I said to Kushi.

"What?" She asked.

"Brides *do* wear colors other than the traditional shade of red," I said, referring to the bride who wore a blush pink embroidered with silver threadwork and Swarovski crystals. It looked stunning, but itchy. I imagined the bride putting her hands behind her back to satisfy that urge. Her updo was adorned by a headpiece of similar extravagance. The groom wore an off-white *kurta-set*, a long top with matching pants and a blush pink vest. His turban was also off-white and blush pink.

We took our seats, alongside our parents, at the table. Amma wore an intricately-embroidered turquoise saree and Khala matched her daughter with a mint green one. Our fathers both wore dark gray suits and striped ties, although of different shades. We munched away on appetizers served at our tables. I was almost beginning to feel calm until that calmness was boxed up and set aside, next to the other wedding presents, only to make room for the most annoying lines of all time, "DID YOU HEAR...?"

I heard it not once, not twice, not even thrice, but just enough times to feel extreme anxiety and outrage. *Bengali elders, like the desperate housewives of hoo-ha, loved their gossip!* I thought to myself. Occasionally, however, the things they said definitely tickled my ear and I couldn't help but laugh. For example, one aunty said to another, "Just the other day, our neighbor was watering his plants, his wife came out in her maxi dress, towel wrapped on her head and as soon as she took that towel off and let loose of her gorgeous long hair, his lungi accidentally loosened a little!" The ladies gasped and clasped their mouths with their hands to hide any hints of amusement. "He caught hold of it before it reached his knees!" Their cackling was contagious. At least their gossip didn't anger me like the ones back at home, in the Bronx, did.

In fact, the very night before we made our way to JFK Airport for our trip to Bangladesh, gossip came knocking on our apartment door, but not before I entered, soaking wet from head to toe. My mother immediately stopped me from walking any further down the corridor.

She went on a rampage about why I always had to walk in the rain without an umbrella. Meanwhile, I found solace in the smell of the incense she had lit around the house to overpower the smell of curry. Amma had just finished cooking and cleaning, she complained. I tried comforting her with the words, "I will make sure to mop the floor." Somehow, those words enraged her because *clean* for me was never clean *enough* for her. My mother was very particular about how things should be organized. I would call her "obsessive-compulsive," but I would probably get slapped across the face for it. Best to keep that comment to myself.

"Asha!" She growled. "Sometimes, I just wonder how you will survive in college!"

"It's okay, *Amma*. Think of it this way, if there is ever a monsoon in Bangladesh, I will be more than prepared for it!" At that point, I was shivering.

"So, you were training for Bangladeshi weather?" Amma asked, looking up at me with her big, gray eyes.

"Yes," I managed to say through gritted teeth, ending it with a hiss. *So, so cold.*

"Well, you've been wasting your time! Monsoon season is over." With that came the calm after the storm. Amma had just dried my hair into a frizz with a towel when the doorbell rang.

She threw the towel onto the nearest heating element and wrapped her orna around her head, a sign of modesty in Bengali culture.

"Hello, Amita," said the other Bengali woman, wearing a flowery maxi dress.

"Hello, Shuzi," Amma replied.

Upon noticing me, Shuzi Aunty said, *"Ya'Allah!* Were you caught in the rain, you poor thing?!"

"Actually, Aunty, I showered in it." I smiled as widely as I could, without expecting her to return it. Her wry face and widened eyes begged me to disappear.

I briskly waltzed down the corridor as I heard her asking Amma for a couple of onions.

"So sorry to bother you. I know you're traveling tomorrow...."

"No, it's no trouble at all. The onions will probably go to waste anyway, as we won't be home to make use of them. You can have as many as you like!"

I heard Shuzi Aunty clap her hands together in pure joy.

Like Shuzi Aunty, there were a lot of aunties and uncles who lived in our neighborhood. We were not directly related to them, but it was Bengali courtesy for me to call my parents' friends by those respectable titles. Overall, there was a close-knit Bengali community in the Bronx. There were advantages and disadvantages to this. I should have found comfort in knowing that if we were to ever run out of salt, curry powder, chili powder, or even water, there would always be a lending hand. However, I despised what was to follow in that very moment:

"Amita, did you hear…?" Shuzi Aunty began.

I loathed every sentence that began with the words, "Did you hear…?" In fact, if I could have, I would have just grabbed those words and twisted them until they choked and could never be spoken again.

I stepped into my bedroom, but to my misfortune, I still heard Shuzi Aunty speaking. "Did you hear that Risa's daughter ran away last night, married a Spanish boy and returned home this morning *with* him? She even dared to ask for her parents' blessing!"

At that moment, I imagined my mother clasping her mouth in utter shock and then inviting Shuzi Aunty into our living room for a cup of chai and biscuits. They probably sat down on our big, plush, velvet sofas. I stayed out of their way lest I should open my mouth and instead of releasing butterflies and flowers, I would spit out wasps and cacti. In fact, my words would have stung Shuzi Aunty to the point where she would go around, spreading yet another wildfire that began with "Did you hear...?" except that time, it would be about *me*. Perhaps she would begin with something smokey like, "Did you hear that Amita's daughter is supporting Risa's marriage 100 percent?!"

Then, that smoke would be ignited to, "Who knows? Even Asha might have a secret non-Bengali boyfriend!" This would ignite the inevitable wildfire that is always birthed from Shuzi Aunty's mind, "He might even be...Spanish! Or...Black! Parents should not give their children so much freedom, I tell you!" And just like that, the sentence that always began with "Did you hear..." usually ended with blaming the child's upbringing, thereby insulting parents.

Little did I know that Shuzi aunty's fire would follow me all the way to Bangladesh. I began to wonder whether or not she had cursed me for my bad attitude that night and that curse was contagious enough to have rubbed off on my cousin.

"What a beautiful couple! *Mash'Allah*," Amma said, the last word meaning "What God has willed" in Arabic.

"Um...what side are we on again?" I asked her. "The bride's or the groom's?"

Khala whispered something into Amma's ear, so she was too distracted to answer me at that time.

Then, Kushi slipped me the invitation scroll. I rolled the scroll open to read the following: *You are cordially invited to the wedding of our son, Ruhul Khanom, to Srisha Haque, the daughter of Poppy Haque and Tushar Haque on....*

"Ah, I see. We're on the groom's side. How do you know him again?"

"He's the son of one of our neighbors; we used to play as kids, but he's much older than I am. He went off to study at Dhaka University a few years back and got a job there. We barely saw him."

"So... basically, we're invited to and sitting at the wedding of a person you barely know?"

"Come on! You must surely know how Bengali weddings work?"

"You're right, I do, but I still can't wrap my head around *why* we do it." What I was referring to was the fact that South Asian weddings, in general, were unnecessarily anything but intimate. An intimate wedding, instead of the unnecessarily big and very public event, might as well have been in a broken down, cold shed, attacked by black crows.

What we, Bengalis, *felt* the need to do was invite almost every single person we ever crossed paths with throughout our lifetime because it's considered rude to have known someone at one point and then not talk to them again, even if it's like 20 years down the line. "People talk," my mother often said. I responded exactly as I did to Kushi, "Who cares if people talk?! I certainly don't." I threw the scroll down onto the table before I realized I was speaking too loudly. I lowered my voice. "We should act like the celebs every time they are the center of attention for the wrong reasons." I waved and smiled at the strange lady staring at me from the table next to us. "We should just *ignore* what people say."

"Is that why you just smiled and waved at that lady?" Kushi laughed. "Because you want to *ignore* her?!"

"Ha, ha," I sarcastically dragged out.

Kushi shrugged her shoulders as the appetizers rolled in. Scrumptious *pakoras* and *samosas*. As I munched away, I heard, yet again, the words, "Did you hear...," which completely ruined my appetite. I looked up to see the strange lady from the table next to us whispering to Khala.

"That young man, over there...," the lady pointed somewhere in the distance behind Kushi and me. She smiled with her crooked teeth, which were marred by betel nuts and betel nut leaves. Her thin hair, parted in the middle, seemed oiled back into a small bun. She looked like she was in her 60s, wearing a cream saree with black and white beadwork stitched into the edge.

She continued, "He's an electrical engineer, got his degree from Chittagong; he lives and works there now, too. He's Srisha's brother. Very smart, very handsome and looking for a bride."

145

Hearing those words, Kushi suddenly looked up at the lady, dropping her samosa onto her plate. She wiped her hands and mouth with a napkin. Then, she robotically took out her mauve lipstick from her clutch. She clicked her phone in selfie mode to see herself in it and meticulously applied lipstick on herself. As she smacked her lips together, a hand tapped on her shoulder. It was Khala who then whispered something inaudible into her daughter's ear. Without giving me a look, Kushi obediently followed her mother and the strange lady. I got up and sat next to Amma. She and I watched them.

"What's happening?" I asked her.

"Watch and you'll probably figure it out for yourself," Amma replied.

"Why can't you just tell…."

She shushed me before I could complete the sentence.

I watched Kushi, who walked just as gracefully as she had done on the first day I met her. Something was different, though.

When I first met her, Kushi wore a school uniform which made her look our age.

This time, however, Kushi wore an anarkali, her orna flowing in the wind, which escaped the outdoors to find sanctuary indoors, and she walked with the confidence of a businesswoman...a *woman*, period.

"Amma...."

"Yes?!" She sounded irritated.

"Do I look older today?"

"Yes, you do. It's probably the makeup and the dress."

"Kushi definitely looks like a woman today."

"Mhm."

That is I could extract in this moment from her.

I couldn't lip-read, so I analyzed their body movements, including hand gestures and facial expressions for the most part.

It looked like the strange lady was introducing Khala and Kushi to a guy and another woman whom I assumed to be *his* mother.

The guy was tall, slim, vanilla-toned and wore glasses.

He looked astute in his white and copper kurta set. His mother wore a brown saree, mottled with mirrors.

Once introduced, all five smiled at each other, my cousin, my aunt, the strange lady, the guy and his mother. Khala and his mother seemed to be getting friendly, talking about...well, I didn't know.

The guy said something that made Kushi giggle.

"Who is that strange lady, and what is she doing with our precious family members?"

My mind ru wild with the possibilities.

"Her name is Khaleda. She's an aunty and... she's a matchmaker."

"Aunty? More like granny, and she's a...what did you just say?"

"A matchmaker."

My mouth fell open, seemingly locking itself in that position. It took some effort to mobilize it again.

Amma mistook my silence for not understanding her: "A matchmaker introduces two potential suitors and their families to one another with the hopes of a successful match as in...."

"As in...for marriage?"

Amma nodded.

"Oh my...."

She covered my mouth with her hand to shut me up. "I know what you're thinking and before you release any wasps from your mouth, let me explain something to you."

I nodded.

She released her hand from my mouth and I rested my head on my hand as I intently listened to her.

"Remember, you asked me to find out more about what's been going on with Kushi, so I asked Joyti if there was anything that I should worry about. There are rumors going around that Kushi has a boyfriend; she's been seen with some guy on a motorcycle a few times around town...in front of their house and so on. Instead of confronting her about it, Joyti and Nil have decided to...well...." Amma pointed to the scene before us, the one where the potential bride meets her potential groom with the hopes of replacing the word "potential" to "permanent."

"And...what did *you* say, Amma? How did *you* respond to your sister?"

"I said nothing."

"But…."

"But, nothing. Joyti didn't ask me for my opinion, so I couldn't give one. It seemed like it was already decided, so it's not my place…it's not *our* place to interfere. This is *their* family and they make decisions together."

"It's child marriage, Amma!"

"Kushi will be 18 in six months, which they plan to be around the time of the marriage."

"To whom, exactly?"

"They have no groom yet. They're putting her out there for the world to see."

I clucked my tongue against my teeth and rolled my eyes. Watching Kushi battering her eyelashes and beaming a toothy smile at a complete stranger who could potentially become her husband made my insides churn. But I knew that the person responsible for putting my cousin in such a despicable situation was the devil in disguise, Josh Costa. *Is*

this the master plan that Kushi said would save her, the one that she
spoke about on the rooftop, the one she intended to set in motion today?

"But, Amma, this is wrong! Their reason for marrying her off is completely wrong! Like, there's no communication between them."

"What if Joyti already asked her? What if this is what Kushi also wants?"

"It can't be! It's not!" I looked into Amma's gray eyes to see some truth in them.

"Last night, Kushi came downstairs and, in front of your father and me, proclaimed to her parents that she was ready to settle down and she wanted them to 'look for her.'"

"Look for her," I repeated.

"She said that? I don't believe it." I shook my head and some petals that were stuck in my hair fluttered onto the table.

"Let it go," Amma demanded. She then shot me *the* eyes, the ones that were wide enough to show me she meant business and the ones I dared to never question.

"Okay," I lied as I admired how graceful my cousin looked, turning around, her orna brushing against the guy's hand as she strutted away and the guy, looking down at his hand that had been brushed by such beauty.

He watched her walk away. There was this big, goofy smile plastered on his face. I wanted to rip that plaster off! I cringed at the thought of marriage at 17 years old.

On the contrary, all I saw ahead of *me* was college, not an exchange of rings, hundreds of guests, nor flower petals falling from the ceiling. *No!* 17-year-old girls were meant to dream much bigger than that and suddenly, I found myself transformed back to the 19th-century character of Jo March from "Little Women" by Louisa May Alcott. Jo would never approve of this; there was so much wrong with the situation; Jo would have stood up for her sisters: Kushi was planning on getting married for all the wrong reasons, her parents were planning on marrying her off for all the wrong reasons, my mother was not giving her own sister advice for all the wrong reasons, my mother was encouraging me not to give my cousin advice for all the wrong reasons.

"This is wrong," I said under my breath, not realizing Kushi had just sat down next to me.

"Did you say something?" She asked.

I looked at her rosy cheeks and glowing smile. "No." It was not the time nor place to discuss all of the wrong things that were happening.

No matter how much the adults were deciding, how much my cousin felt the need to be her own vigilante, how much I needed to mind my own business, I wasn't going to…and for all the *right* reasons!

The strange lady introduced herself to me. "I'm Khaleda. You can call me 'Aunty.'"

"Salam, Aunty...how are you?" I greeted.

"I am well, Dear. Sorry, I didn't know that Kushi had a cousin from America visiting."

Yes, and I bet you're just as ecstatic as I am repulsed by the thought of you matchmaking me with some random guy.

"What do you do in America?" She asked me.

"She's studying in high school," Amma replied. "She will start University soon."

Shoo, Aunty, shoo!

"Oh, wow," she replied. "You will be on your own then, all alone?"

"No, actually, she will be close to home, so there is no need to move out," Amma replied.

"Wonderful. Your mother will still be cooking for you, then?"

I waited for Amma to answer for me as she had been doing, but she just stared at me.

"Um...yes, Amma is an incredible cook."

"Do you cook?" Aunty asked me.

I burst out laughing in front of everyone at the table, my parents, Kushi's parents, and Aunty.

I was sure she would get the point and leave me alone right then and there.

Rather, she said, "What a beautiful smile she has!"

O-M-G.

Amma nodded and looked at me with her serious, intimidating eyes again.

"Well, answer your aunty's question!"

"What quest...oh! Do I cook? Um...I can put bread in the toaster. I also burnt myself once making tea."

I grinned, satisfied with my answer. *That should eliminate me from her plans.*

She winced, probably unimpressed enough to move on to the next potential bride. "Maybe, it's time you learned," she said.

"Actually, Aunty, I was hoping my future husband could teach me."

She gasped. Kushi coughed excessively after having gulped down water into the wrong pipe. Khala nearly choked on some rice. Amma let her eyes seethe through me, but I refused to let it burn. Khalu and Abba blatantly ignored us and got up to go to the restroom.

I took a bite of my roasted chicken before looking up to notice Aunty had disappeared. I smiled, completely satisfied with that fact. I looked at my cousin, whose eyes were locked with those of her potential suitor's eyes. They smiled at one another from a distance as I grimaced and smacked her arm.

"Ouch!" She cried, drawing attention to herself.

"What do you think you're doing?!" I yelled, drawing even more attention to our table.

"I'm enjoying my meal," she dragged out as she picked at her rice with her fork.

"You're flirting with that guy," I whispered.

"It's called 'being nice.'"

"Well, you could've fooled me! Your 'being nice' is more like a 'come-hither' signal.

You're batting your eyelashes at him and practically inviting him to come over to our table. Before we know it, he'll be showering you with compliments and you'll be blushing, hoping nobody would notice under all that makeup and then...and then...there'll be an exchange of flower garlands and rings, and there'll be a whole stage set for you two!"

"When you put it that way, it sounds...."

"Like a nightmare?"

I clenched my fists under the table, squeezed my fingers in tightly like snails finding protection from this war within their shells. Why couldn't Kushi see what I saw in her? I saw a young girl whose dreams were just meager seeds, planted within the soil of her heart and mind, only growing roots for something bigger than...larger than a bridal throne and for what? For whom? For that son-of-a-...for Josh?!

Kushi's words shattered my thoughts into an infinite number of glass shards, "You were a little girl once, Asha."

"I still am," I replied through clenched teeth. I loosened the fingers of my fists a little. This was me, waves receding after a tsunami. "Last I checked, you still are too. *We* still are little girls, Kushi." *Do I need to slap you across the face for you to understand that fact? Recede, Asha...recede back into the tranquility of the ocean. Breathe. Breathe. 10-9-8-7-6....*

"Even so, didn't you ever dream of meeting the one someday and getting married?"

"I used to play 'pretend wedding' with my dolls if that counts?"

"Let's say those dolls were your subconscious self. What color dress did your doll wear on its wedding day?"

"Pink...because I didn't have any white doll-sized clothes."

"What did their wedding look like?"

"It was fun, I guess, for a 'pretend wedding.' What's your point?"

"Asha, this is the norm here."

"Why does everyone keep telling me that?!" And by "everyone," I meant my mother and Kushi.

"Because it's the truth.

As soon as a girl reaches a certain age where her parents believe she is mature enough for marriage, they will start looking for a potential groom for her. They usually start early because it can take months...*years* to find 'the one.'

This little introduction

between Salim and me is just that, a *little* introduction. I'm

not getting married tonight, Asha. I barely know the guy."

I tried to find some roses in her words no matter

how many thorns there were in them, thorns of the false

notion that her parents believed she was ready for marriage,

that *she* believed she was ready for marriage when in fact,

neither of them believed she was ready for marriage at just

the age of 17! In reality, they were trying to escape a horror

movie where the viewer screamed at the screen, "Don't

open that door! Don't open that door!" Yet, Kushi and her

parents opened that door and behind it was either some

random guy like Salim or some demon like Josh! They were

basically doomed! What hurt me more than those thorns

pricking away at my heart was the fact that I had no idea

what Kushi was going through, that my *knowing* some of the

facts only made me feel more and more helpless. And yet, I refused to completely give into that feeling when this beautiful, graceful, kind girl deserved to see her seeds grow roots long enough to birth jasmines and marigolds; she deserved more than the stagnant seed, famished and thirsty inside the soil; she deserved just the right amount of the sun's rays, taking turns with the rain.

"Ouch!" I felt a pinch on my shoulder. Kushi hushed me, a petrified expression written all over her face. But a motorcycle inside a wedding venue would be impossible. So, what was she so afraid of? I followed her gaze onto a man, a woman and a young man who could pass as their son. The woman had short, wavy hair, highlighting the red dot on her forehead and she wore an exquisite, threaded black and beige saree. She was adorned with gold bangles and necklaces. The man wore a black suit, beige shirt and black tie, most likely having planned to match the

162

woman. I gathered they were husband and wife. He was a bit pudgy and nearly bald. The rings on his fingers had exotic stones on them. And the son had on a slim-fit black suit with a maroon shirt and striped skinny tie. He smiled and smoothed his gelled hair back as he spoke to his parents and then pointed at me...no, not at me, at Kushi?

"He looks so familiar," I whispered.

"It's Josh," Kushi whispered back.

"WHAT?"

"Shhh!"

"Sorry. It's just that he looks so...so...."

"Decent?" She tried to finish the sentence.

"I was going to say 'normal,' but 'decent' works too. Oh no, he's walking over here!"

By this time, our fathers had joined us. Everyone, including Josh, Kushi and I, exchanged *Salam*. Our fathers looked overly joyed to be having a conversation with Josh's parents. *They really must be well-known*, I thought to myself. Tanshara, Josh's mother and our mothers exchanged polite conversation about her saree and her fashion design house in Dhaka. My father and Khalu exchanged cordial conversation about Raj's furniture business and the USA. Like most Bangladeshi families, Raj Costa also had relatives all over the world, including in New York City. Meanwhile, Kushi, Josh and I said nothing.

"This is our son, Josh," Tanshara introduced.

Upon hearing his name, Khala's smile completely disappeared. She recognized the name from the marriage-proposal letter to her daughter, which she had found in their mailbox, the one that Kushi had claimed was just a prank. Khala then locked her eyes with Kushi's. Her pupils, I imagined, burst into flames, while Kushi's, I noticed, were glazed enough to be a potential fire extinguisher for the flames. I imagined what Khala could have been thinking at that moment: *Had Kushi been keeping her relationship with Josh a secret from me this entire time? Had Kushi planned on having Josh ambush Nils and me at the wedding so that we could officially meet her groom-to-be? Who is this girl who claims to be my daughter?!* I almost didn't notice Kushi get up and flee the scene. She was headed toward the restroom and I intended to follow until I heard Khala yelling at Tanshara.

"Are you aware that your son sent a fake marriage proposal for our daughter in our mailbox?" Khala asked.

"I'm sorry?" Tanshara said, thoroughly confused. "I got his letter asking for my daughter's hand in marriage. I hear all the boys are playing pranks like that on the school girls."

"Wait just a minute," Raj said. "Let us explain."

"You're all in on it?" Khala asked.

"Our son is genuinely interested in marrying your daughter," Raj said.

"What?!" Khalu said before Abba calmed him down.

"Let's hear them out."

Tanshara said, "Josh asked us to come forward with the marriage proposal. We had other brides in mind, but he wants Kushi. We didn't know he wrote you a letter until after he had done it. He got a good lecture about how improper that was. We apologize on his behalf for the letter." Tanshara turned to Josh. "Son?"

"I'm sorry," he murmured.

An awkward silence followed. The flames in Khala's eyes turned into a forest fire.

Khalu seemed at a loss for words, which shocked me. All I could think about was when we first landed in Bangladesh and Khalu showed me how to firmly communicate with Bangladeshi customer service. Yet, there he was, at a wedding venue, getting a marriage proposal for his daughter from a prestigious family, all the while... getting screwed over.

"Forgive his innocence, please," Raj pleaded.

"Innocence? Your son is...how old is he?" Khala asked.

"24," Raj replied.

As their point fingers flew up in the air like shotguns, the adults debated about what made a marriage proposal appropriate or inappropriate, what made a man interested in a girl, appropriate or inappropriate, and whether or not their marriage would be appropriate or inappropriate considering the rumors about their relationship. Meanwhile, I watched Josh's smile vanish, his mouth shut tightly, most likely holding swear words hostage at the tip of his tongue and his fingers strangling one another. Josh transformed from "decent" to "demon" within seconds. He speed-walked toward the restroom. I

167

followed him as quickly as possible through the crowded venue.

As soon as Kushi came out of the restroom, I saw Josh grab her by the wrists and push her against the wall. He whispered something under his breath, each exhale blowing away loose strands of her hair from her face. She closed her eyes and whimpered from the excruciating pain she felt from his attack.

My eyes searched frantically for a solution, which led me to taking off one of my sharp-heeled shoes and aiming it for Josh's back. *Bullseye!* He yelled in pain and let go of Kushi, who ran toward me. He slammed his fist against the wall and went into the men's restroom. As soon as he was gone, I grabbed my shoe, put it back on and escorted Kushi to a safe space.

I said, "I texted you a few times, asking you if you were okay."

"I left my phone at home," she replied.

"I was going to try to find you sooner, but I wanted to stick around and listen in on what the parents were discussing...for your sake."

"I understand."

I looked down at her hands.

"You're bleeding!"

She presented her arms to me.

Beneath the chiming of her bangles were the screaming of crimson nail marks embedded into her skin. I took a tissue out of my clutch and wiped away the blood with it.

She held the tissue tightly against her skin as I asked the waiter for a first-aid kit which he brought right over.

"I hope nobody sees the band-aids," she whispered to me.

"They won't see them under the bangles, Sis."

I held her hand tightly and led her through the crowded venue just as she had once held mine and led me through the crowded bazaar. We sat down on vacant seats, waiting for the flames at our reserved table to simmer down. There was a moment of silence; we were each lost in our own thoughts. All I could think of saying was, "I love you, Sis."

She finally smiled, and replied, "I love you too, Sis."

I put my arm around her and I held her.

"Thank you," She said.

"For what?" I asked.

"For being here."

This was one of *those* kinds of moments, the kind I wanted to screenshot with my mind.

As we walked through the flower tunnel back to our car rental, my parents, my aunt, my uncle, Kushi and I were silent. *This was good because uttering the slightest word about* *the drama that had just ensued would only spark anger and resentme*nt, I thought to myself. We were about to get into the car when we noticed the motif of a motorcyclist against the sapphire night sky. He had on a helmet and a leather jacket. Just when we ignored him, thinking it couldn't possibly be Josh as Josh was wearing a suit that day, the man approached us and handed Kushi her phone.

"You dropped this, Madam," he said.

She accepted the phone and he left immediately afterward.

"Didn't you say you left your phone at home?"

"I did say that."

"Why did you lie to me?"

"I didn't lie."

"So, you did leave your phone at home?" I asked.

Kushi nodded.

"Then, how did it end up here?"

She just stared at the phone in her hand.

I inhaled the cold night air as deeply as the volume of what I had come to realize. "Josh? He has the keys to your house or something like that?"

After releasing a long, quivering sigh, Kushi answered, "Something like that."

She sounded tired, tired of being followed, tired of being watched, tired of being harassed, tired of being manipulated, tired of being abused. I prayed she wasn't too tired to fight back.

"Kushi, this is…."

"Yes, Asha, it is."

"I mean, he's…."

"Yes, he is."

"And we have to…."

"Yes, we do."

OK!

"I'm glad to hear you say that." And by "that," I meant that we were going to fight back. I hoped she really understood me.

That night, back at the house, Abdul asked once again if we wanted to hear a horror story. Kushi sped off to her bedroom.

"Thank you, Abdul," I replied. "But, I think we've had enough horror for tonight."

He just gave me a blank stare before he noticed my parents and Kushi's parents entering the house, exchanging angry whispers.

I darted upstairs before they could see me.

Sometimes, I woke up feeling like I was really awake when I was actually in another dream! That's why I thought I was experiencing a nightmare within a nightmare when I seemed to be falling into an abyss until I hit my mattress and woke up, only to find a hand gripping my mouth shut. All I saw was a dark male figure and I smelled the musk on his neck as he whispered into my ear in his raspy voice.

"She used to be a good girl," he said. "She used to listen, she used to answer as soon as I called her; she used to let me take her out. But then, you came along and she's completely changed."

I felt his grip grow tighter and tighter until it hurt and I struggled to breathe through my already-blocked nose. My allergies had taken a toll on me recently.

"You listen to me carefully, now. If you keep messing with her head, I'll mess with yours until it bursts and you become nobody."

With that, he let go of me and I gasped for air as he phantomed away. When I got up, I ran to turn on the light. Then, I noticed *Frankenstein* staring at me from the bedside table and I wondered whether or not what had happened, actually happened…like for *real?* Could Josh have actually been in the room? I opened the book to sift through my pencil-marked notes, to see if I could find the object that manifested itself in the form of a nightmare: "*A fiendish rage animated him as he said this; his face was wrinkled into contortions too horrible for human eyes to behold….*" Suddenly, I heard the raspy voice again. When I looked around the room, there was nobody there. I was completely alone, except for *Frankenstein* and his "fiendish rage."

CHAPTER 6

THE NIGHT CREATURES

I remembered when the coconut palms tried to whisper something to me, through the wind, during my trip from Dhaka to Sylhet before the bus driver nearly killed us. Well, I was finally going to decipher their secret! Kushi's parents and my parents felt that we needed a getaway from the drama with Josh and his parents. I was super excited to rediscover my mother's birth village, her childhood home and the school she had attended. I was only a toddler the last time we visited *nanabari*, a Bengali term meaning "grandfather's village from the mother's side."

As we neared the village, I felt like I was in an H. G. Wells novel. I noticed that the wilderness of city streets transformed into the spines of crop fields. The binding of rooftops became the umbrellas of palm trees. The line of flower pots became the winding legs of banyan trees. The only consistency there was, was the sun in its red glory, lighting the pathway home. *Home.* At least, that's what it felt like for me, having been away for years, rediscovering it all.

Kushi and I wore simple pastel-colored cotton salwar kameezes. I wore a blue one to match my nose ring. Kushi wore a pink one and made sure to pick one with long enough sleeves to cover the evidence of Josh's fury on her wrists. I reminded myself why I didn't just pull her sleeves up right then and there to show the adults in our lives the true nature of the devil; no matter how much I wanted to divulge Kushi's little secret, it wasn't just hers to keep anymore; it had also become mine! It had become *our* little secret and one that bond us closely enough together that we had become more like sisters than ever before; basically, I wanted to stay loyal to the sister I never had. I gathered that Kushi didn't tell her parents because she still believed that they wouldn't understand. Regardless, I decided that we could fight Josh together, just the two of us, Kushi and I. I did successfully attack him with my shoe, after all! A smirk sneaked up at the corners of my lips.

"What are you smiling about?" Kushi asked.

I hoped my smile didn't reveal my thoughts.

I replied, "I'm just excited about all of this! It all looks so serene, like the perfect

escape."

"Escape," Kushi whispered in a matter-of-fact manner.

She opened the window, and the wind instantaneously began to tackle our ornas, almost pulling them off our necks. I begged her to close the window. She did, saying, "Not so serene, after all, eh?"

I rolled my eyes at her. "Are we there yet?" I asked Abba, who was sitting next to the driver.

"Almost!" He replied. "I feel like we're on a road trip to Niagara Falls. You were so little back then and kept asking every few minutes if we were there yet!"

Amma added, "And every time we came to a rest stop to snack or eat, we appreciated how you were too distracted to ask us if we were there yet!"

"Interesting. I don't remember it that way. I do, however, remember getting two or three happy meals!"

"Oh yeah, of course, you'd remember that!" Abba said, laughing until we came to a sudden jolt. The car had stopped.

"Are we here? Are we here?" I asked, fidgeting in my seat.

"No," Abba drew out.

I frowned.

"There's a woman standing in the middle of the road," he said.

We looked out of the front window and saw a frail woman in an orange saree, her hair up in a messy bun and a wide toothy smile on her face. Upon seeing her, Khala replied. "Ah, I recognize her!"

"You do?" Amma asked, not seeming to recognize her at all from their childhood at the village.

"Everyone, let's get out of the car," Khala replied.

"What, why?" I asked no one in particular. We followed her out and approached the woman.

Khala handed her some cash.

The woman slipped it into a small pouch.

She then picked up a musical instrument resembling a flute.

"It's called a pungi," Kushi replied.

"Oh, so she's going to perform for us?"

"Something like that," Kushi smirked.

As soon as the woman began blowing into her pungi, the lid of a small cylinder basket suddenly began rising.

I immediately took a step backward, bumping into Kushi, who held me by the arms and smiled.

Together, we watched a snake rise from within the basket.

It appeared hypnotized by the woman...no, by the tune she had been playing! It swayed from side to side. Impressed by the performance, I thought about how unbelievable it was that a venomous reptile could so easily be manipulated! I wondered if this woman played another tune that controlled human beings. I knew for a fact that we, humans, were certainly mesmerized by this street show.

I clapped my hands together like I was five years old again and attended a dolphin show at the aquarium.

I wanted to ask the hypnotist about the secret to her tricks. *Perhaps, we could use them to take down Josh?*

As soon as I was about to approach the woman, Amma grabbed my hand and led me back into the car.

"You are not petting another filthy snake, young lady!" She yelled.

"I wasn't going to pet the snake! The idea didn't even pop into my head, but now that it has…."

"Hush!"

I giggled.

In about three minutes, Kushi said, "We have arrived, Sis!"

I was excited to arrive at destination.

Stepping out of the car, I saw a turquoise mud house topped with a thick tin roof.

There was a lake nearby and farm animals, including lambs, chickens and cows. There were small children running up to us, welcoming us. One of them whispered, "Do you have a gift for me?"

Kushi shooed them away with her hands.

"That's kind of rude, don't you think?!" I said, taking my purse and side bag with me.

"Around here, you need to be a little mean. Otherwise, it'll be too hard to flick them off your skin like little blood-sucking mosquitos. They will suck you into pity."

"I have cash…." I had a feeling our neighbors here, in the village, were going to be poor and in need of charity.

"Yes, but remember what I said when we went to the bazaar?"

"Don't pass money out until it's time for us to leave?"

Kushi nodded, dragging a wheeled suitcase behind her.

We walked into the house; there was beautifully-carved wooden furniture everywhere and colorful cushions. A woman in a sky-blue saree welcomed us.

"Come in, come in! Ay, Kinthu, come and help with the bags!" She called out to a boy, seemingly in his pre-teens and wearing a checkered shirt with jeans. He said, "Salam," before throwing my bag over his shoulder. "I'm Saya," the thin woman said. "Look at how big you've grown!" She smiled warmly at me and pulled me in for a hug before abruptly pushing me away.

I noticed Khala walk in behind us with a big pot of meat and my mother following closely behind with a bag of rice. Amma had explained that we were going to cook our meal together and then take a nice promenade through the village.

A jolly man walked into the house just as we were sipping our chai. He had a basket full of fish of varying sizes. His name was Golpo, also a Bengali term for the word "conversation."

"Hello, I am Golpo, husband to Saya," he said with his hand on his chest. "You can call me Uncle."

"Nice to meet you," I replied. Kushi explained that Saya, Golpo and Kinthu were distant relatives of ours. Golpo offered to pour us some more tea. Abba, Khalu, Kushi and I respectfully declined, asking for cold water instead. After serving us four glasses of water, Golpo sat down on a small straw stool and discussed the good ole' days with the men, everything from their childhood swimming lessons and fishing at the lake nearby, milking goats, pretend-fighting with broken branches to dancing in the rain.

"Abba, this is nanabari, so how is it that you knew Golpo as a kid?"

"I grew up in the neighboring village. We had common family friends, your mother and I."

"Will it rain today, you think?" I asked Golpo.

"Yes. It is already cloudy. We need the rain; otherwise, it will be too dry for our crops and livestock. We don't want another drought."

I barely heard his last few spoken words. I was too busy thinking about the rain. I smiled so widely that everyone looked at me with quizzical eyes.

As our mothers and Saya cooked, Golpo took us out to the coconut palms. I looked up at the coconut palm leaves, like hands reaching out to us, yearning for company...for friendship.

We can share secrets, I said to them in my head. *I can start. A monster is haunting my cousin and I feel helpless. Do you have any advice?*

Kushi pulled me back as a coconut fell to the ground at the very spot I had been standing. I finally noticed Golpo at the top of the tree, a rope supporting his waist and his legs hugging the bark while his hands extended an offering of friendship to the coconut trees, or so, that's what I imagined he was doing.

Well...? I hoped the coconut palms heard me speaking to them through my thoughts and could give me some words of wisdom. I had read somewhere that palm trees could live up to a century. A breeze whisked up the bottom strands of my hair, brushed them against my cheek and then released them just as quickly as it caught them. It tickled my cheek, so I giggled. I looked at Kushi, who was already sipping coconut water.

"Try this," she said, handing me the light green coconut with white inside.

"Mmm, it is so good."

Noticing Kushi crunching in her eyebrows, I asked, "What's wrong?"

"Oh, I think I felt a raindrop on my forehead."

I smiled a big goofy smile. Before Kushi or I could say another word, the downpour caught us by surprise. Everyone ran onto the porch to take cover, everyone...except me. I couldn't move. I put the coconut down on the ground, closed my eyes, stretched out my arms, and tilted my head back until I met face-to-face with the cloudy sky.

Is this it? Are the coconut trees trying to tell me not to worry by summoning the rain, which I yearned for? Has Bangladesh finally accepted me as its own?

I could hear Abba yelling, "Come back in. You're going to get sick!"

"Bhai," Golpo began, "We should just join her and relive our childhood memories!" He released a hardy laugh, but the men did not join me. Kushi did, though!

Holding hands, we turned around in a circle, laughing and dancing. I couldn't help but feel like *this* was exactly what she needed after what she had gone through...was *still* going through!

As soon as the shower stopped, Saya ran out with fresh towels for us and led us back inside, where the meal was ready to be served. We changed into dry and brighter salwar kameezes.

After the meal, we took that walk our mothers had promised us. The rain had stopped, and the red sun shone. Strolling along the crop fields and passing our neighbors, we were in the spotlight...or rather, sunlight. The villagers must have sensed that we were newcomers...foreigners and for some reason, I felt offended by such unspoken thoughts. I didn't want to be seen as a newcomer, nor did I feel like one. We came to a small, narrow, blue building. Through the windows, I could see that there were classes in session, children in sky-blue uniforms and teachers in either shirts or sarees.

"I went to school here," Amma whispered, her gray eyes glistening in delight.

"Wow." There was something magical about standing on the very ground my mother had been educated on as a child, where she had learned how to read and write, and where she had eaten her lunch with her friends. I looked at my mother, whose eyes were searching again for those moments long gone, those teachers and friends she had said "farewell" to, those classmates she had played with during recess, and the tranquil landscape that surrounded the school and created the perfect study ambiance.

"I can't describe the feeling of being back here. I just...miss it."

I couldn't imagine what it must have felt like for my mother, who had left the only home she had ever known, to immigrate to a strange land and start her life from scratch again. She was like a saree, unstitched only to be restitched in a whole new color, a whole new style and a whole new size of experiences. I respected her for making the best out of a change she probably didn't like very much at first. I respected her for adapting to a foreign land while still maintaining her culture. I admired her. And then it hit me...I would soon be leaving high school and venturing off to university.

Kushi held my hand. I could sense she was unhappy and probably needed to talk about *it. How is it possible that she still looks so stunning with a frown on her face? My face is the ugliest when I cry!* We sat together under a banyan tree, its legs ready to dig us up from our deepest sorrows.

"10 days, Asha. I only have 10 days left to give Josh my answer."

"Oh, right, Josh's ultimatum." I sighed, holding her hand even tighter. "Your answer will be 'No.'"

"But...."

" 'No.' You will tell him, 'No, I am not going to marry you.'"

"You have no idea how risky that will be...the stories I've heard...the articles I've read about girls in the same situation as I am; you have no idea what happened to them and their families...."

"I *do,* actually. I did some research last night before going to bed. It gave me nightmares. It only makes me want to take the risk more. *We* will take that risk and everything is going to be okay." I tried to sound more confident than I actually felt.

"How can you be so sure?" She wiped away some tears with her orna. "He can be dangerous. He's thrown me off his motorcycle and he's done other things like...well, like what you recorded with your phone...."

I took in a deep breath and closed my eyes. "There's something about this place, Kushi. I just can't explain it, but there's something that tells me we are going to figure it all out *together*."

When I opened my eyes, I saw Saya swoop in with a basket full of snacks, warm chicken samosas, shiny green packets of spicy potato crackers and glass coke bottles, the kind you see in those 1950's American commercial ads. Saya's saree flew against my face and I got a whiff of *curry* odor. I winced at first but then realized how hungry I truly had been.

"Thank you, Saya, you have been working so hard today."

"Anything for you, Dear. I missed you." She sat beside us. "Have you ever heard the story about your mother and this tree?"

"This...t...tree?" I asked. Fear hopscotched over the goosebumps on my arms.

Saya nodded.

Kushi was about to look up when I warned her not to, paraphrasing the story that Abdul told me about my mother, the creature possessing her and the exorcism.

"I suddenly don't want to sit here anymore...." Kushi whispered.

"Me neither," I whispered back.

"Oh, please! Trees aren't cursed! These creatures go where they want, *when* they want, and it has nothing to do with just ONE place," Saya said, like what she had said

194

was the most normal thing in a most normal conversation. *That* disturbed me. *Creatures? Should I "Bah humbug" this? Hmm...that didn't end so well for Scrooge in* A Christmas Carol *by Charles Dickens.*

With that thought, we heard footsteps approaching us from behind. Kushi and I pounced on one another. *Creature?!* Once we saw that it was just a little girl, we sighed again with relief.

The girl had her silky hair pulled back into a long braid, tied at the end with a white ribbon.

"Is it true that you're from America?" The girl asked us

"Yes, *I* am," I answered.

She smiled. "Is it true that your mother went to our school when she was little?"

"Yes, it's true," I replied.

195

Her smile grew wider. "What an honor! Can I sit with you, Apa...Apas?" *Apa* is the Bengali term for elder sister.

"Sure!" Kushi and I made space for the girl as Saya began packing up our leftover snacks.

"What's your name?" I asked her.

"My name is Tanshara, Apa." She took a sip of her juice.

"Do you like attending this school?"

"I love it! It's just...the most wonderful place. Sometimes, I learn things that I can use to help my family, like how the water pumps and irrigation system work!"

"Wow! What do you want to be when you grow up?" I asked.

Her honey-dew eyes lit up in the sunlight. Then, just as quickly as they lit up, they grew very dark. I saw her hunch over and get lost in the shadow of the banyan tree.

"Well…," she began. "I had always dreamed of becoming a doctor and going to medical school in India or America. I hear India and America have the best medical schools."

"That sounds wonderful! How old are you, Tanshara?"

"Fourteen, Apa."

"You will be off to medical school sooner than you know it, then!" I tried to smile so widely that it could be contagious. But it made her frown more. *Was my smile that ugly?* I looked at Kushi, who solemnly looked off into the distance; she was lost in her own thoughts, staring at two kids dragging along four goats that had ropes tied around their necks. The irony of the scene made me shudder.

"I'm not going to medical school anymore," Tanshara said. "I have new dreams now, *other* dreams that can help my family."

"Can we hear about them?"

She took out her phone from her backpack and showed me a picture of a man. His smile appeared forced, reaching only his cheeks but not his eyes. *Joy can be seen in one's eyes*, I thought to myself. *And this man did not look joyful.*

"Is this a picture of your father or uncle?" I asked her.

She choked on her juice. "No, Apa." She croaked before clearing her voice. "That's my husband-to-be."

Her words, "husband-to-be," pulled my eyes wide open. "You mean, your fiance? You're engaged? As in...you're getting married?"

She nodded.

I nearly dropped her phone but caught it and handed it back to her. I didn't want to see the photograph anymore, let alone touch it.

"This new dream you have, what is it exactly?"

"To be a good wife and mostly, to be a good daughter to my parents."

"Those are beautiful dreams. I have only gotten to know you, but I'm sure you are already an excellent daughter. As for being a wife…you have so much time to settle down. Why do you feel the need to rush it?"

Tanshara merely shrugged her shoulders.

I looked back at Kushi, who was now looking straight at me. She seemed almost possessed and I was beginning to suspect that the creature my mother had seen as a child was dangling its legs above us. I dared not look.

The girl continued, "What is most important is that my parents and my little brother get to keep our home, get enough food to fill their stomachs with and enough medicine to heal them when they are ill." It seemed like a rehearsed speech she had been telling herself over and over again. She smiled that same smile her fiance had on *his* face in the picture, the one that didn't reach her eyes. All Kushi and I could do was smile back with pity in our eyes.

I held the girl's hand and said, "Don't give up on your dream of becoming a doctor even after...even after...." I couldn't bring myself to say it: *marriage. How on earth is child marriage allowed? Aren't there laws to stop it here? And if there are, what's being done to enforce them?* I was determined that I needed to do some research on this when we returned to the city.

"Will you two come to my wedding?" She asked us and it took me by surprise because as much as I wanted to say "No," I wasn't sure how to let this sweet little girl down.

"Oh," Kushi finally spoke. "Thank you, but we are leaving tonight." In a way, I was relieved that this answer would suffice. Yet, I was worried for Tanshara's sake. In many ways, Kushi's situation and Tanshara's situation were alike: both thought marriage was a means of escape from their horrendous circumstances and both thought that in tying the knot, they would be protecting their families. Of course, I was a firm believer in that no child should have to sacrifice their childhood, no child should have to feel like they need to grow up faster than time permitted, and no child should have to give up chasing the end of rainbows to stop at the startline.

"My wedding is in two hours! You can make it, I'm sure." Tanshara looked at us with glowing eyes and we nodded, not wanting to break her already-tarnished heart.

"Appi!" A little boy called out from a distance. *Appi* is another Bengali term commonly used for an elder sister. "*Ammijaan is* getting mad; you need to come home and get ready!" A boy in a flowery shirt and jeans shorts yelled.

"I have to go, Apas. My mother sent my brother to walk me home. I hope you come. See you soon! Salam!"

"Walaikum assalam," we both chanted back before looking at each other, frowning again.

I felt like I was time-warped into the 19th-century and I suddenly remembered a quote from *Pride and Prejudice* by Jane Austen, which I recited out loud, "It is a truth universally acknowledged, that a single man in possession of good fortune, must be in want of a wife."

"Huh?" Kushi commented.

"It's a quote from a very famous and classic book. Tanshara's situation reminded me of it, but I thought we were past the 19th-century way of thinking."

"What about *my* situation? Which quote does it remind you of?"

"Abba gave me a beautiful framed quote once; it's a daily reminder for me and I only now realize how much I needed to see it. The Prophet Muhammad said, 'Whoever treads the path toward knowledge, Allah will make easy for him/her the path to Paradise.'"

"It's beautiful, but I don't hear how it relates to me." She rested her chin on her fist and looked at me with curious eyes. I wanted to shake her, to yell at her, *WAKE UP. How could you not see how it relates to her?!*

"Kushi," I began. "If you don't understand how it relates to you, then you're more lost than I thought you were." I was too angry to look at her. I got up and stomped back to our mothers, who were resting on a blanket beneath another banyan tree. Their ornas spread out across the olive-tinted grass and their arms covered their eyes from the sun's rays. I told them about our informal wedding invitation and they gave us the okay to attend. Of course, I didn't say anything about the bride's age or fiance. That was information that worried me so much that I wouldn't wish that kind of dread on anyone else. Either that, or I was just too afraid of the possibility that my mother would say the words, "This is normal, here," again. I noticed Kushi had already started walking back in the direction of the house. I asked Khala to take a photograph of Amma and me in front of her old elementary school. This would be the perfect image for my next blog entry, which I would dedicate to my beautiful mother. I wanted to spread positivity and show the beautiful side to Bangladesh rather than the ugly side.

The night was dark despite the sky being lit up by 1 septillion stars, that's 1 with 24 zeros following it. The sun had long since set. There was no evidence of rain returning. So, I began to question what Bengalis said about *these* kinds of weddings, the non-rainy, non-sunny kind, the kind of weddings that happened only in the night. *A dark wedding?* I asked myself. *Would it be considered auspicious or suspicious?*

"You don't need to be so glamorous for the village wedding. Just go as you are," Amma said and I trusted her because she used to live in the village, after all. Our parents refused to let us walk in the dark alone.

"The night creatures may be lurking," Saya said. There was no humor in her tone. "Golpo can accompany you."

Night creatures, I thought to myself, were going to eat up Tanshara, not us. *Night creatures* were the misfortunes and circumstances of living in poverty; they were the things that told children an education was okay up to a certain level and then it was time to throw in the towels; *night creatures* were the older and wealthier men who married younger and impoverished girls just to take advantage of them, *night creatures* were… stalkers. I cringed at that last bit of contemplation.

We stumbled onto loud folklore music playing, to which a couple of women in sarees, bright jewelry and bangles danced in circles. They waved their hands up in the air and swayed their hips from side to side. We saw a group of children run past us. Kushi and I recognized the boy. We asked the boy whom we saw calling out to Tanshara at school earlier that day, "Where is your older sister?"

"Follow me," he said.

"I'll wait out here for you," Golpo said, watching the dance performance.

Kushi and I nodded and followed the boy into the house. He was so quick on his feet that we had to jog after him until we came into a narrow corridor. He pointed to the ragged curtain, where a door should have been, as an entrance. The boy ran off before we could ask him to announce our arrival. Kushi and I looked at one another, not wanting to intrude by entering unannounced.

"Tanshara, it's us, the girls you met today at your school. May we enter?" I asked with my mouth as close to the curtain as possible.

No one responded.

"That's strange," Kushi whispered. "I heard a rustling noise inside."

We decided to lift the curtain a bit but only noticed the pegs of a bed. As soon as we entered, we did not see Tanshara. Rather, we saw a wooden bed, mosquito nets hanging above it and flower petals mottled at the center of a colorful bed cover. Next to the bed stood a woman who muttered something inaudible under her breath. All three of us froze and looked at each other. This woman looked Hispanic, mid-thirties; she was plump; her frizzy hair was tied up in a messy bun; she wore safari clothes, an olive green t-shirt underneath a brown leather jacket, on top of a pair of khakis. She held a shiny, black motorcycle helmet against her hip.

"Hello," she drew out, fixating her hazel eyes on us, ready to move the second we pounced on her. But, we had no reason to pounce on her...yet.

"Hello…?" We managed to say back, really wanting to ask, *who are you, what are you doing here and where is Tanshara?*

"How do you both know Tanshara?" She asked us, her chin up, arms tensed. She seemed protective of the girl.

"We just met her today," I replied.

Noticing my accent, she asked, "You're not from around here, I see."

"Neither are you, by the looks and sound of it, no offense."

"None taken…. Are you from an organization?" She asked.

"What organization are you from?" I asked, narrowing my eyes. Meanwhile, Kushi just gave the woman a blank stare.

The woman handed us a card, which read: *Estella Ambrosio, Co-Founder, Wings BD.*

"Listen," she began. "I understand you're both here for the same reasons as I am, but I got this covered. She's already waiting for me out back. I'm going to help her run away and we'll take care of her. If you have any questions, just give me a call."

With that, she crawled out through the open window but poked her head back in one last time. "By the way, great undercover attire!" She meant our salwar kameezes. I thought to myself, *what else would we be wearing?!*

I slipped the woman's business card into my bag as Kushi and I ran to the window. We heard that low, familiar rumbling before it vroomed off-- a motorcycle! Wrapping her arms around Estella's waist as she drove off, was the dark figure of a little girl. The girl's hair seemed braided and ornate with white jasmine flowers. It took us a minute to realize that Tanshara, the child bride, had escaped her fate in a shimmering red saree that battled the wind behind her.

"Wow..." was all I managed to say.

"Yeah..." was all Kushi managed to say.

We both looked at each other in awe as if we had realized something for the first time.

"I so want to be like Estella Ambrosio. She's just...she's so...."

"Cool?" Kushi tried to finish off my sentence for me.

" 'Heroic' is more like it!"

"Let's get out of here before someone comes in and thinks we helped Tanshara escape!" Kushi yelled.

On our way out, we noticed Golpo sitting with his legs crossed on the grass. He was half-asleep.

As if awoken after a nightmare, Golpo asked, "Is the wedding over already?"

"Yes," both Kushi and I said simultaneously. Kushi had rediscovered her smile.

As we walked away from Tanshara's home, we heard a scream in the distance. We turned around to see that there was a row of cars that had arrived outside of Tanshara's home. The jeep in the front was decorated with fresh, colorful carnations. It must have been the vehicle that the groom arrived in. We noticed a crowd buzzing around, wondering what had gone wrong. But Kushi and I secretly knew that everything had, in fact, been set just *right*. And yet, my cousin was no longer smiling.

"What's wrong, Kushi? This is good news!"

"Yes, it is for Tanshara's sake, but her parents...her little brother...who will take care of them?"

I took the business card out and showed it to Tanshara.

"Estelle Ambrosio will take care of them, I'm sure of it. I think we should visit the organization tomorrow. What do you think?"

"Yes, it would give me some peace of mind knowing that a mother and father had not just lost their daughter and that a brother had not just lost his sister."

Secretly, I hoped that this organization could help *us* figure out what to do about Kushi's own night creature.

"Wait," I stopped her from walking. "Do you hear the coconut trees rustling their leaves?"

"Yes?"

The rain hit the ground, marching like an army returning home from a victorious battle.

"The cows got married. It was beautiful," Golpo muttered. We walked closer to him and noticed that his eyes were closed. *Had he been sleep-walking and sleep-talking?* "Chickens and goats were the best guests for dinner." He had definitely been sleep-walking and sleep-talking! Kushi and I giggled as we tried to wake him up. At our village home, we saw our parents packed up and ready, waiting for us by the vehicle.

Saya and Kinthu bid us *farewell* as they held up Golpo, one on each side.

We thanked them for their lovely company and went off on the long ride back to the city.

Upon returning to my cousin's home in the city that night, I could not sleep.

It wasn't entirely because my brain was still running the marathon from the day's events.

I mainly could not sleep because I was still afraid that the nightmare I had the prior night would return and I was even more terrified at the possibility that the nightmare wasn't really a figment of my imagination at all, that it could have possibly been a *reality*.

I opened my social media accounts, something I promised myself I wouldn't do during my vacation.

But I had been missing my best friends. I got a lot of messages from them:

Rachel: I was training with my bike today and I kept thinking about the time you almost ran into me with yours! I miss you, girl.

Maria: Mom made spicy tacos. You missed out big time! What am I missing out on? Tell me how you're doing!

Angel: I'm so close to figuring out a real-life murder mystery, but I need your help! Call me!

Noreen: Are you alive? If you are, reply to me! Also, please, please...don't come back as a married woman! I know some girls that went back to South Asia and ended up either staying for good or returning as married women!

I was so tempted to tell them about Kushi and Josh. However, due to cultural barriers, only Noreen would've understood. And I couldn't tell Noreen because some things were best kept secret between sisters. So, I replied to each one with the exact same message:

Asha: I miss you, girl! I'm alive! I've just been having a great time getting to know my relatives and the people of Bangladesh. The red sun here is the best escape from the cold weather. It's so inspiring. I wish I could give you all of the details of my visit, but then there'll be nothing left to talk about when I get back! In the meantime, keep checking on my blog for new posts and pictures as often as you can! Love you!

And then, I took out My Little Tanzanite, skimmed through my scribblings, opened up a laptop and entered a new blog post:

Prophet Muhammad (peace be upon him) said, "Paradise lies beneath the feet of your mother." I now understand why. My mother and I visited her old elementary school today. It felt incredible to see her face light up the way it did and not just because we were under the red sun! It felt amazing to be standing on the same ground as she did when she was a young student. Looking at her longing eyes, I realized how much she had given up when she left her homeland; she left behind memories that we dusted off the dirt roads in her childhood village today. She sacrificed coconut trees for oak trees, crop fields for concrete sidewalks and left her parents so that she could provide for them better in a more prosperous environment. Once she became a parent, herself, that's all I could see...Amma. I never really asked her about her childhood, where she came from, how she felt when she moved countries or how she met my father. This trip has given us an opportunity to connect on a whole new level, on a pathway to paradise, God willing.

CHAPTER 7

THE HESITATION

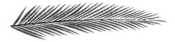

A tall, gray, concrete, rectangular building stood before us. The grass and bushes were embroidered with fresh, vibrant blooms.

A pond was nearby, small frogs hopping from one lilypad to another, zigzagging their way around the water lilies.

"The water lily is Bangladesh's national flower," Kushi explained.

"Cool fact!" I said.

217

She held her phone against her chest. "Nine days left," she whispered.

I put my guiding arm around her. "We will figure it out. Now, let's see what this organization is about."

Upon entering, we saw a large sign with the words "Wings BD" on it.

To our right was a receptionist in a blue and white saree, neatly wrapped around her waist and folded over her shoulder.

She had a blue dot on her forehead and dark lipstick. Her hair was up in a bun. She looked young yet professional.

"Welcome to Wings BD. How may I help you?"

"Oh, we're here to see Estella Ambrosio."

I handed her the card Estella had given to us. I hoped it would be our ticket in.

"What are your names?"

"I'm Asha and this is Kushi."

"Do you have an appointment, Madams?" She asked.

"Is that what your organization is about? Making appointments?" I asked, thinking back to how Khalu had said we needed to be firm and demanding when we wanted something done. "I thought you were all about helping people...helping young girls. We are two young girls who are here, seeking help. If we can't get to Estella, we demand she come see us!" The receptionist looked bewildered. I lowered my voice and said in my most gentle tone, "Tell her that the two girls she met at Tanshara's wedding want to see her."

"One moment, please."

I think it worked.

The receptionist called over the security woman in a turquoise uniform shirt, badge and navy blue French hat. She whispered something inaudible into her ear as we nervously waited, anticipating the possibility that we could be thrown out.

The guard scrutinized us up and down, perhaps to decipher whether or not we were trustworthy enough to get through security.

Kushi and I had on jeans and colorful tunics. The officer nodded at the receptionist and walked over to us.

"How did you get Estella's card?"

"She gave it to us last night, at the village, when she rescued Tanshara from...child marriage."

"So...Mitha says you are here seeking help? Refuge?"

"Mitha?"

"The receptionist."

"Oh, Mitha...we didn't have the pleasure of exchanging introductions!" I said, nervously giggling. "We aren't *seeking* help...well, we are, but to ask about...about your volunteering opportunities!"

Kushi gave me a look as if to say, *shut up before you say something stupid.*

"Yes, volunteers are always welcome here!" She replied. "I'm Onthara, Head of Security at Wings BD."

"Nice to meet you, Onthara; I'm Asha and this is my cousin, Kushi."

Onthara gave Mitha a thumbs up and signaled to another female officer to take over her spot while she guided us through the security check and up two flights of stairs.

On our way up, she asked, "How old are you?"

"We're 17. I live in America and Kushi lives here, in Sylhet."

"The girls here will be so excited to meet a volunteer all the way from America!"

"How long have you worked here?" Kushi asked Onthara.

"Three years, but the organization has been around longer than that. We help girls who experience abuse, either psychologically, emotionally and/or physically. Some come to us on their own, but mostly... *we* find them. Wings BD is a non-profit organization, a sort of safe haven, a home away from home for girls who suffer from injustices of abuse and/or child marriage." Her back was turned as she spoke robotically.

It sounded like she had repeated the same speech to newcomers more times than she could count.

The first floor had a row of doors, possibly small rooms. A little girl in a puffy dress peeped her head out from one of the doors and said, "Salam." We returned the greeting with "Walaikum assalam."

"What happened to her?" Kushi asked.

"You mean, what *didn't* happen to her?" Onthara replied. "We rescued her just as we did the girl last night...child marriage." The girl had two braided pigtails and she was very short. She looked like she couldn't have been older than 10 years of age. I was so inspired by the organization that the thought of volunteering during the rest of my vacation sounded like a great idea! Not to mention, it would count as volunteer hours I could put down on my college applications. I wasn't sure Kushi was up for it, though; she had been too stressed, too busy figuring out how to survive her own battle the next nine days. One of our SAT words in high school was "clandestine," which perfectly described *my* intentions with coming to Wings BD in the first place. We needed allies in the war against Josh Costa.

When we arrived at a door that was slightly ajar, Onthara turned around and we finally got to speak to her face-to-face. Her dark eyes were the friendly kind and her smile seemed genuine.

"Here we are, Estella's office. She's inside, and she signs on all volunteers and staff. Judging by the fact that her door is ajar, it means she's free for drop-ins. I'll wait out here in case you need me."

"Oh, you don't have to wait for us," I said.

"I know, but it's actually protocol around here for new visitors. I'm required to wait here."

"Okay...." I drew out and knocked twice on the door.

"Come in!" Estella said from within. She sounded cheerful.

Her office was classic...antique. There was cherry brown wooden furniture everywhere, a plush brown leather therapy divan, a wide and tall brown leather desk chair, and a large rectangular desk. Across from the desk were two chairs that looked like they were from a dining room table set. They also seemed to be anticipating our arrival.

"Please, have a seat," Estella insisted, not looking up from her laptop.

She seemed and looked different, completely engrossed in her work and wearing a gray suit and a pink shirt. Her professional attire was a shocking contrast to her safari outfit.

Working woman by day, superhero by night.

"Oh, it's you two!" She said when she finally looked up. "From another organization!"

"Actually...." I began but couldn't get myself to say it.

"Actually...what?" She asked, narrowing her eyes at us.

I looked over at Kushi who seemed to be depending on me to do the talking.

225

"There was a misunderstanding last night. We're not from any organization."

With that, Estella slid her laptop aside, folded her hands on top of her desk, leaned forward, and shot us an intense gaze. "My job is to protect Tanshara and girls like her," she began. "So, if you two don't have that same goal, then you need to go. Onthara!"

The officer came in and said, "I see you've met our new volunteers."

"Volunteers?"

"We're here for the same goal as you are," I quickly said with a teeth-revealing smile.

Kushi nodded vigorously in agreement.

"Oh...well then, volunteers are always welcome," Estella enthusiastically proclaimed.

Onthara walked back outside to guard the door as Estella picked up her office phone and rang reception:

"Mitha, three cups of chai, please. Are you okay with milk and sugar in your tea?"

We nodded.

"Yes and…." She paused before continuing, "Tell Ishitha to come by my office."

After she hung up, Estella said, "So, let's begin with the tour."

We followed Estella to two large doors inside her office.

As she pushed them open, they revealed a balcony. The balcony overlooked an emerald and jade garden.

There were girls in puffy dresses and salwar kameezes swinging on wooden swing sets that dangled from tree branches, playing tag with one another, jumping rope, tossing balls around and exchanging conversation.

A woman came out with a tray full of fresh fruits. The girls immediately surrounded her.

"It's snack time," Estella explained. "Every morning, the girls wake up at 7:30 sharp. They have their lessons before this break. Then, they go back to classes before lunch break. And finally, they end their classes around 2:00 p.m., after which they are free to do any other activities they wish on the grounds of this facility.

They are allowed to leave the grounds on weekends, but there is a sign-up sheet for that, as we have a limited number of drivers and security working with us.

They are never allowed to leave without protection. We have a trusted team of teachers, police officers, counselors, cooks, cleaning staff and volunteers starting at age 16.

Each person is given a contract, a tour, instructions and training with a detailed understanding of what their roles are at Wings BD. We like to think of each other as members of a big family."

It bothered me a bit that she didn't say a big *happy* family. I suddenly noticed a girl whose face looked like it had been melted...sagging. She ate a slice of mango alone on the grass and as far away from the other girls as possible.

"What happened to *her*?" I pointed her out to Estella.

"That's Karishma. She's an acid attack survivor. She came to us last year and had just turned 14 years old last week. She likes to keep to herself. She's an introvert."

"How did it happen?" Kushi spoke for the first time to Estella. "How was she attacked?"

"Karishma was being stalked by a man whose advances she rejected. Her stalker decided to take revenge and throw acid on her face one morning when she was walking home from school. We found her at the hospital and brought her here."

"Did the guy ever get caught?" I asked.

"Yes. We found him not long after the attack and he was arrested. Onthara!"

With that, I noticed Kushi close her eyes and release a sigh of relief.

Onthara joined us on the balcony. For the first time, I noticed how relaxed she was in her posture with us. I had always imagined police officers to be stiffer.

"Yes, Estella?" She asked.

"Question. What happened after Karishma's attacker was arrested?"

"Oh, he was released. I went back to find him at his home, but he wasn't there. I assume he's moved away to avoid confrontation with police around here."

"So... he's still out there?" Kushi asked, probably imagining it could possibly be Josh they were talking about.

"Unfortunately, yes," Onthara said. "I understand it's disappointing and frightening as he's dangerous and still out there, on the streets, somewhere, but Karishma is safe as long as she is here." That was another thing that worried me, the fact that she was *still* here after a year and would still be here, most likely for a very long time...too long.

"What about her family?" Kushi asked.

"Her family...isn't very accepting of her anymore, to put it delicately," Estella explained.

I knew right then and there what she meant. Her family had disowned her because she didn't look like the "average" girl.

They thought more about their own family reputation than about the family itself. I had read many articles and blog posts about these kinds of attacks, the consequences and why girls like my cousin suffered in silence.

"People talk," Kushi had once said.

"People talk," Amma had once said.

"What are the chances that if a victim seeks refuge here, their attacker will be caught and justice will be served?" Kushi asked.

"Chai, Madams." Mitha laid the wooden tray of an intricate golden tea set, down on the table.

We all sat down. She poured us each a cup. I picked up a biscotti.

"Onthara, would you like a cup of chai, too?" Estella asked.

"No, thank you. I'll be heading back to my post."

After Mitha left, Estella asked, "Sorry, what was your question again, Kushi?"

"What are the chances that attackers get caught and arrested?" She rephrased in a harsher tone.

"Unfortunately, low. But, we really *do* try our best."

"I don't doubt that," I said and took a sip of my chai. It tasted just like the one Abdul and Zulekha usually made. Yet, at that very moment, not even chai calmed our nerves.

"Our main goal here is to provide food, shelter, education, protection…a *real future* for these girls.

That is a promise we can and will always fulfill."

I offered Kushi the plate with biscottis on it, but she just shook her head.

"Is there something on your mind?" Estella asked her. I assumed, after years of experience, she saw in Kushi's eyes that something was wrong.

Kushi asked Onthara, "What made *you* want to join Wings BD?"

"*Ahem.* Nobody other than Estella has asked me that question before."

"If it's too personal, you don't need to share. I understand."

I was also curious.

"No, it's okay. I've learned to tell my story without tearing up. I've also learned that sharing it can impact others *and* me in a positive light." She gave Estella a firm nod as if it were Estella who taught her that. "My ex-husband was okay with me working after marriage, but he wanted to approve the *kind* of job I chose. I realized that last bit too late. I had already joined the academy a few days before our wedding ceremony and when I told him about it on our wedding night, I was expecting him to be overjoyed by the news. Instead, he was infuriated. He said, 'That's a man's job. Even if you could do the job, you would be surrounded by men. It's inappropriate. I don't approve.' When I made the point that our prime minister was a woman, surrounded by men, keeping law and order, he didn't like it because he knew I had a point. He took his fury out on me with his fists. I left the next day and I came here. Wings BD helped me recover, find a home and a support system. *This*," she pointed to her badge, "is my way of giving back to the organization."

Her eyes were not teary. Rather, they looked off into the distance as if she could still see it all before her eyes, the hurt and the pain. Perhaps, it was a memory that was farther and farther away but still visible. I looked up in sheer admiration of this Bangladeshi woman who was in uniform, strong in both physique and mind. Onthara then returned to her post, guarding the office. A woman leaned against the doorframe of the balcony. She had a long braid and wore a white lace salwar kameez.

"Hello, Ishitha! I want to introduce you to our two new volunteers, Asha and Kushi." We got up from our seats and shook her hand as Estella continued, getting up from her seat. "This is Ishitha, one of our trusted counselors. I have some work I need to tend to, so I will leave you two in good hands for the rest of the tour."

We followed Ishitha back inside the office.

Before we could exit the office, Kushi turned around to ask Estella, "How is Tanshara doing?"

The room became tense at once.

"You will most likely see her during your volunteer hours and get the opportunity to ask her yourself."

Kushi didn't budge.

Estella sighed. "Tanshara's fine. She's missing home, but she's fine."

I looked over at Kushi to see only hints of worry in her eyes. I knew that we had to meet Tanshara, in person to help Kushi realize that this organization could be good for her, too. There was an aroma of jasmine in the corridor. We entered a room with ten empty chairs set around in a circle at the center. It looked like a counseling session had taken place or would take place at any time.

I wondered how they began their meetings, something along the lines of :

Hello, my name is Tanshara and I am a victim? Hello, my name is Tanshara, and I was a victim? Hello, my name is Tanshara and I'm a victim of child marriage?

"Here, we have our weekly counseling sessions. This is just one of the many rooms we use. We meet a group of girls who share similar experiences. Volunteering here means that you have to understand and be ready for the harsh realities that the girls bring in here from out there and I warn you; it can be psychologically and emotionally draining. Even I, as a professional, am unable to sleep most nights. You will be meeting with girls who have almost given up on life, girls whose friends have already taken their own lives, girls who experienced every kind of abuse and torture possible: some left traumatized, speechless, have burn marks or scars, among other non-visible and visible injuries. Some of the girls can even be intimidating or violent, so you need to be prepared to listen and to think *first* before reacting."

Gosh, no sugar-coating it…at all. For a counselor, she didn't seem positive or even…hopeful.

Karishma walked into the room. Behind her was another girl, shorter and younger than she.

"We are about to start a session now. You can join us, but don't speak. Just listen for today. Consider this a trial session for you to understand whether or not you are ready to take on the task of volunteering here," Ishitha explained.

By the time we sat down in three of the seats, the other seven had already been filled.

Soon the chatter came to a halt and things started.

"Welcome, everyone. We have with us today two new girls who will not speak but will be listening. This is Asha and next to her is Kushi," Ishitha said.

"Welcome, Asha and Kushi," the girls seemed to sing simultaneously.

"Would anyone like to share how their day is going so far?"

"Lunch was disgusting," a little girl said.

We giggled.

"It tasted like a rat's tail," she said.

"Have you ever tasted a rat's tail before, Aariya?"

"No, Madri, I haven't, but I imagine that's how it would taste."

"You know what I heard in all of that you just said, Aariya?"

"What?" Aariya asked Ishitha. The girl seemed irritated by Madri's comment.

"That you have a wonderful imagination!"

Aariya smiled and blushed. "Thank you."

"You're welcome. Anyone else would like to talk about their day?"

"Today is the anniversary of...of...." A teenage girl began. I noticed that she had small cuts on her wrist.

"It's okay. You can say it."

"We're here for you," some of the girls said and continued to encourage her.

The teenage girl, whose shawl was covering half her face, said, "Today is the anniversary of my husband's death."

"Is that really what the anniversary is celebrating, Humaira?" Ishitha asked.

Silence beckoned us and we let it swoop us away for a while. This was a chance for the teenage girl to think...to remember.

After a few minutes, Humaira began talking again. "No...today is the anniversary of my survival and we will celebrate that."

"I think you should share your story again with us, Humaira."

Why was Ishitha pressuring her?

For the first time during the counseling session, the girl moved the shawl to reveal two small scars on her left cheek. She told her story:

Two years ago, Humaira was on her way to school when a man stopped her in her path. He offered her some chocolate. When she declined, he got angry and used one hand to push her cheeks in tightly enough that her jaw was forced open. He used his other hand to stuff the chocolate into her mouth. "Chew," he commanded. She saw his eyes immediately soften as if he found pleasure in watching her suffer. She was afraid he would do more than just touch her cheeks. But he didn't. Instead, he walked her to school every day. He often teased her. Sometimes, he took her into alleyways and touched her body in places she didn't want to be touched. She wanted to tell her parents about it, but he threatened to cut their throats if she did. Eventually, her father heard from neighbors that his daughter had a "secret boyfriend," who was really a grown man. He decided to follow her one day to see if what the neighbors had said was true. Ashamed of what he saw, he decided that the best way to get rid of the shame was to marry his daughter off to that very man. Humaira protested, telling her parents the truth, but they said it was too late, that things had gone too far and she needed to honor their reputation. Thus, after a year of being followed, Humaira got married to her stalker and abuser.

On their wedding night, her husband suddenly found the urge to cut her. She had been sleeping when he took a knife to her left cheek, hence the scars. She woke up screaming from the pain of the attack, ran to the bathroom to mend her cuts, and came out with a pair of scissors behind her back. Her husband had been asleep when she stabbed him. As it was self-defense and she had agreed to undergo a psychiatric investigation, Humaira called Wings BD her new home.

After having told the story, she looked straight up at Kushi, who was shivering.

"Are you okay?" Ishitha asked her. "Would you like some water?"

Kushi did not reply, so I spoke up for her. "Water, please!" What I really wanted to say was, *Of course, she's not okay! You were supposed to give her hope and instead, you crushed it!*

After drinking the water, Kushi and I left the room to get some air. Ishitha followed closely behind, asking over and over again if Kushi was okay. Kushi obviously wasn't, as she couldn't even get herself to respond. I didn't answer Ishitha because I was just so infuriated with her! Nothing she could say could console us after having listened to Humaira's story. What kind of a counselor was Ishitha? She obviously didn't prepare us well enough for this! *Was she trying to discourage us from volunteering?* I wondered. *Who throws volunteers into the most difficult task on the first day?! Why not just give us a tray of fruits to pass around?!* But then again, I thought to myself, Ishitha did not say or do anything wrong. She had just told us and shown us the truth-the "harsh realities." We just could not handle it.

There we were, staring at the ground on which we stood, the one that resembled nothing close to the one my mother was educated on at the village.

My mother was educated on a ground full of innocence, but this ground was full of *experience*; girls here had seen the darkness of the world far too early in life, far

244

beyond what my eyes could comprehend and far out of what my heart could take in.

A girl in a long braid, tied together with white ribbons, stopped in front of us. She held Kushi's hand.

"Apa?" she said.

As if lifted from the ground, we looked up to see a concerned Tanshara. We threw our arms around her.

"I'm okay; I'm fine," she said.

"Are you, really?" we asked, not noticing Ishitha had snuck back into her counseling session.

"I am just fine. I've even made some friends and the teachers here are so nice; everyone is welcoming. My room is comfortable too. Estella says that here, they can really help me become a doctor! I can accomplish my *real* dreams while my family is provided for."

That was when I knew, in my heart, that "harsh realities" could lead to something as positive as the beaming smile on Tanshara's face and as inspiring as Officer Onthara.

Those were the faces I kept envisioning over and over again until we stepped out of the CNG outside of Kushi's gate. We heard the familiar noise of a dog barking in the distance. When the barking sounded more vicious and closer in proximity, we looked in the direction of the source of the ruckus. It was running toward us at such a speed that it almost caught up to our feet by the time we ran inside the gate and shut it behind us.

"Cute dog," I whispered, panting and pushing my back against the gate as Kushi locked it.

The barking sound was muted by yet another familiar noise: a motorcycle whizzing past the gate. Kushi and I immediately looked at each other and we didn't even have to say his name to know that it was, indeed, *him*.

"It was *his* dog," Kushi said, panting.

Just then, Amma, Abba, Khala, Khalu, Zulekha and Abdul ran outside of the house.

"What happened?" Khalu asked.

"What...what do you mean, Khalu?" I asked, patting my chest in an attempt to slow down my heart.

"We heard you screaming," Abba said, holding a book in his hand.

"Um," I laughed nervously. "It was just a dog."

"Oh Shuna, I don't understand how you pet snakes but are afraid of dogs," Amma exclaimed.

"Well, I'm just glad you're okay." With that, Abba buried his nose back into his book, which reminded me, I needed to catch up on "Frankenstein."

Everyone returned inside the house just as quickly as they had run outside of it. On my way inside, I noticed Abba sitting in the living room next to the bookshelf. He had discovered the incredible collection of books by Bengali

247

authors like Humayum Ahmed, Rabindranath Tagore and Sarat Chandra Chatterjee. On my way upstairs, I noticed Khala whisper something into Kushi's ear, upon which Kushi's eyes widened like a moon flower that only blooms in the dark. Shrugging my shoulders, I grabbed my copy of *Frankenstein* from my room and returned downstairs.

Abba looked up from his book and smiled at me before diving right back into his reading. I sat across from him and opened *Frankenstein* to one of my annotated pages: *"Scoffing devil! Again do I vow vengeance; again do I devote thee, miserable fiend, to torture and death. Never will I give up my search until he or I perish; and then with what ecstasy shall I join my Elizabeth and my departed friends, who even now prepare for me the reward of my tedious toil and horrible pilgrimages!"*

It got me thinking. *Something unjust was happening to my cousin and I wanted to save her, but would that be considered an act of vengeance when all we would be seeking is justice?*

248

CHAPTER 8

THE PROMISE

"Amma…" I whined.

Her "mom-look" shut me up.

We had gotten ready in our best salwar kameezes, the kind that had pearls and crystals sprinkled all over them. The girl who was the most extravagant for new guests at the house was Kushi. She wore a regal pink saree embroidered with similar designs as our salwar kameezes, except hers had heavy silver threadwork lining the border. She made her hair into a curly updo. She looked…grown up. I could feel my blood pulsating like lava as I watched my cousin adorn herself with jewelry for a strange man who could potentially become her fiance and, later, her husband.

"Are you sure about this?" I asked Kushi in front of Khala and Amma. I wasn't sure why I did, expecting very well that she would lie about her feelings in front of them. I guess...I secretly wished our visit to Wings BD, having met Tanshara and Officer Onthara, had inspired her enough to become a fighter, to speak out loudly about what she really felt, to stand up for herself... to seek help.

"Of course, she's sure," Khala replied for Kushi, whose eyes said otherwise. Just then, I wished I had on safari clothes, a helmet inhand and my own rescue ride waiting outside of my cousin's gate. I wanted to save her from the slightest possibility of marrying a man just to escape the wrath of another man and, most of all, making a commitment too early in her lifetime. Of course, we still had time to figure it out. We had nine days left and today was not her wedding day; rather, it was a second, more formal introduction between two families who could potentially unite due to matrimony. *Potentially. Potentially. Potentially.* I kept telling myself that to remind myself of how nothing was set yet, of how there was still a chance for my cousin to escape this *and* her stalker. *Just an introduction. This is just an introduction. Vengeance. Vengeance. Must seek vengeance.* Out of nowhere, *Frankenstein* crept into my brain again. If my cousin wouldn't fight for herself, I would definitely like to fight for her!

Before we walked down the stairs, I noticed Kushi looking at her phone.

"Is there something wrong?"

She ignored my question and said to everyone, "I need to use the bathroom. Kushi can bring me downstairs."

"Bring you downstairs?" I asked.

"It's tradition. She can't enter alone," Amma said.

"Why not? Is it bad luck or something?"

She shrugged her shoulders. I was grateful she didn't reply with that's just the norm around here.

Khala eyed her daughter up and down suspiciously. I guessed she wanted to make sure that Kushi wasn't a runaway bride...but, she wasn't a bride yet. I sighed and reluctantly followed Kushi.

The next thing I knew, she was on the rooftop, standing at the edge.

I grabbed her arm and pulled her back. We lost balance and she almost toppled over me.

"What are you doing? Let go!" She screamed before straightening out her jewelry.

"No, I refuse to lose the only sister I ever had!"

"What are you talking about?"

"Well...weren't you going to...?"

252

She just stood there and looked at me. "Wasn't I going to…what?"

"What are you doing, then?"

Kushi whispered, "Look down."

Holding hands, we both neared the edge. Lo' and behold, there *he* was, perched up on his Having trouble with indentation here... motorcycle, like some animal instinctively alert. He took off his sunglasses and picked up his phone. Kushi's phone seemed to be screaming his name as "Josh" appeared on the screen. Josh heard her phone ringing and frantically looked around for her.

"He…hello?" She whispered so that he could not figure out her exact location.

Speaker, I mouthed, but she shook her head and pointed over the edge, a signal that meant she could not put him on speaker lest he should hear it and know she was up there. I shook my head with pity. My cousin had become a prisoner in her own home by none other than a power-hungry, possessive maniac. And why shouldn't she feel that way? After all, he could come inside and leave as he pleased, with or without a key.

"Mhm." She mumbled something and hung up.

"Well? What did he want?" I whispered.

"He wanted to hear my voice…."

Before she could continue, she made sure Josh had left.

"That's it? He came all the way here to just hear your voice?" I asked.

"He said in case I didn't pick up the phone, he would *figure out* another way to hear my voice."

"He was threatening you, basically."

She nodded. "And…he just wanted to hear my voice, so he drove past the house in case I didn't pick up."

That was a close *call,* though, no pun intended. The guests would soon be arriving. We could not risk any more drama than there already had been in Kushi's life.

"So, that's what he thinks a relationship is like?" I began to wonder what kind of monstrosity he must have experienced in his own life, growing up, that he turned into this...*thing.* His parents seemed normal enough, but then again, many things happen behind closed doors that we don't always get to see or hear about.

"Asha...." Kushi began but did not continue. She began shaking.

Her eyes told me she had no idea what to do with herself anymore. She looked over the edge of the rooftop and I decided to walk close enough to it to block that view. *No, she couldn't...she won't, and I will make sure of it.* Kushi was like a rat stuck in the dead end of a maze with no way forward and only one way back, only to hit her nose against yet another dead end. *I will help her break that wall, and we are going to make it through this. I just wasn't sure how. Vengeance! No...justice! Yes, justice.*

In the meantime, we walked down the stairs into the living room, an array of laughter and colors. The potential groom's side had adorned the coffee table with dishes and trays of *mishti* or Bengali sweets, samosas and other snacks and gifts. The trays were all wrapped in colorful transparent gift-wrapping paper. Kushi had one end of her sari on her head, looking more and more like a bride than ever. Putting a shawl or saree on one's head was a sign of modesty according to Bengali social decorum. Everyone exchanged polite greetings and small talk. When we were finally seated, I looked at the family sitting across from us. I remembered them from the wedding we had recently attended. The bride and groom looked at Kushi and whispered something inaudible to each other, smiling adoringly at her. They were Ruhul Khanom, Kushi's neighbor and his wife, Srisha Haque. Shrisha's parents, Poppy and Tushar, were also present. Shrisha wore an extravagant saree, matching in the same color as her mother, mauve. Both Tushar and Ruhul wore kurta sets with golden waistcoats. It seemed we weren't the only ones over-dressed. Yet, I found that visible fact repulsing; I didn't want to look anything like that family. I wanted them to think we were so different that they'd get scared and run off. The presence of betel-nut-eating and greasy Khaleda Aunty, the matchmaker, irritated me. She smiled at me, seemingly impressed by my traditional attire. I imagined she was thinking, *Any guy would love to snatch this traditional Bengali-American, their ticket to life in America!* Little did she know, in America, 17-year-old Bengali girls are often encouraged by their families to further their education and think of marriage later.

"Forgive our son, Salim. He's having an online meeting with his team back at Chittagong, but he will be joining us soon," Poppy, his mother, said.

"Yes, of course, we understand," Khalu replied. "I'm Nil and this," he pointed to Khala, "...is my wife, Joyti." He then introduced the rest of us to them.

"How are you, Kushi?" Tushar asked.

"I'm doing well," Kushi replied.

"I hear you're studying and planning on continuing your studies even after marriage?" Poppy asked.

Why don't you just ask her what she's interested in? Why the need to go directly to studies? I grew suspicious.

Kushi nodded her saree-covered head.

"That's impressive, and you should know we have no issues with that," Poppy said.

There it was! The bait Poppy most probably thought would hook my cousin and draw her into their family. Why couldn't families just assume that would be the case without the need to highlight it beforehand, like some sort of a contract that needed to be signed? Kushi forced a smile as they continued.

"I, myself, am training to become a teacher," Srisha said, nodding her head vigorously. "What do you wish to study in the future?"

"Architecture...like my father," Kushi replied.

I studied the family's facial expressions. Khaleda Aunty's grimace revealed she was *not* impressed. However, Salim's family seemed indifferent to Kushi's response. I wasn't sure whether or not that was a good thing.

Apart from *Frankenstein*, I had read too many horror stories the night before, biographies of young girls dreaming of education and careers but being married into families who promised them that they could continue their education, only to end up enslaved. I even tried finding laws that could protect my cousin against her stalker and against her potential groom, but I found nothing. More than half of Bangladesh's girls married between the ages of 15-18. Kushi would soon become one of those girls. I could try to accept that not all families are the same and that Salim's family's promises could possibly be genuine.

However, after everything that Kushi had gone through, all I could think about were these lines from *Frankenstein: "Follow me; I seek the everlasting ices of the north, where you will feel the misery of cold and frost to which I am impassive. You will find near this place, if you follow not too tardily, a dead hare; eat and be refreshed. Come on, my enemy; we have yet to wrestle for our lives; but many hard and miserable hours must you endure until that period shall arrive."* I was lost and still, I was not willing to accept that we had, indeed, lost.

Khala, Amma, and Kushi got up and went into the kitchen.

Just then, Salim walked in. He matched Ruhul and Tushar. They had blatantly planned this.

Salim seemed to be taken by Kushi's entrance. She gracefully walked in, carrying a tray on which was a tea set. She put it down on the coffee table, not looking up at anyone. I wasn't sure why she averted her eyes so much. *Was she afraid that they would reveal her true feelings about all of this? Was she nervous about locking eyes with her potential fiance? Did she think that if she noticed her surroundings too much, it would all seem more real to her than she wanted it to be?* She poured the chai into each cup and served it, starting from the eldest who was present, Khaleda Aunty, then to Tushar, to Poppy, Ruhul and Srisha. She started to pour the chai for Salim when he interrupted.

"There's no need. I will pour it for myself," he said, almost touching Kushi's hand in the process. She spilled a little bit onto the saucer as a result.

"Sorry," she whispered, still not looking up at him.

"It's okay," he said. "I'll take it as it is."

As Kushi handed him the cup on the saucer, their hands touched again. The cup stopped rattling and Kushi met his eyes for the first time since the wedding. She had obviously been awoken by his touch. I watched in complete shock at what was happening. Nobody else had noticed. Everyone else was busy sipping on their chai and munching away on mishti. Kushi got up and sat down next to me.

"Won't you have some?" He asked.

"No, thank you," she replied.

Her body jittered against mine. She had already been touched by a man whom she despised with every fiber of her being and had now been touched by another man whom she barely knew. Touching between opposite genders was a big deal in Bengali culture. Touching meant sparks, desire...passion. What Kushi was going through was the complete opposite.

"Are you okay?" I asked, knowing very well that she wasn't and hoping that she would admit it...at least, to me!

She just nodded and looked down at her hands.

After the tea, Poppy and Tushar requested on Salim's behalf that he and Kushi speak alone for a moment. Of course, my parents suggested that I chaperone their meeting. I was happy to protect my cousin as much as I could, even if it meant being a third wheel on their first date. I led Salim and Kushi upstairs to the rooftop. I hoped the heat of the sun would boil and cook Salim enough that he would become discouraged and leave. He shaded his eyes with his hand and took out the chair for Kushi. *We will not be seduced by your feigned chivalry!*

He offered me a seat too, but I politely declined, deciding to stand, watch and burn right through him with my eyes. *Feel uncomfortable...feel very, very uncomfortable.*

"Um…" He fidgeted around in his chair a bit. He looked at her with his big brown eyes, poised, wanting to complete his sentence. Then, I noticed how long his eyelashes were; I had never seen a man with such long eyelashes before; he was what one would call a "pretty" boy, hair slicked back, shoulders back and neck high. Even standing as far away from him as I was, I could smell his musk *attar*, a Muslim perfume. It killed me to admit that Salim was, indeed, a looker. I immediately looked away. "Um, is this your first time?" He asked Kushi.

"What do you mean?" She asked.

"Is this your first match meeting?"

How many have you had, Mr. Chivalry? I thought to myself.

"Yes, it is," she replied.

Awkwardness surrounded us like a murmuration, ready to swoop us up into their flock.

"You?" She finally asked him, looking him straight in the eyes this time. He had broken the ice and she had fallen through it.

"I think every relationship deserves to start off with honesty, so I'll be frank. I've had about two potential match meetings thus far, but I didn't feel like we were compatible enough to be a successful match."

Relationship? This was just an introduction, not a relationship! My hands formed fists.

"Oh...well...thank you for your honesty," Kushi said.

"You're welcome," he replied.

Abdul brought three glasses of mango *lassi* and a plate full of samosas up. I gobbled one right up and realized how famished I had been.

"So…never mind," Kushi began before taking a sip of her lassi.

I felt like I was watching a really bad romantic movie which I wanted to switch off.

"So…," she began again. "You're an electrical engineer?"

"Yes, I work with devices that are run by electricity." He took a sip of his lassi. The heat was getting to him, so he picked up a napkin to wipe away the sweat dripping down his forehead.

"You have to be really good with your hands, then," she said, making Salim choke on his drink. "Are you okay?"

"I'm fine," he croaked out. "I guess one has to be pretty good with one's hands, yes."

"What do you like about living in Chittagong?"

"The beaches; they're incredible. You'll love it there," he said in a matter-of-fact manner, which took Kushi and me by surprise. She hadn't even said "Yes," to the marriage proposal and he was already talking about the future. "I mean," he clarified, "You'll love it if you ever visit." *Whew*, he wasn't confirming the match, either.

Just then, gray clouds swallowed up the sun and rain knocked on our heads. *Thank you, God!*

Salim and I ran inside while Kushi was still outside, standing on the rooftop, getting completely soaked. She faced the sky and smiled at the clouds with her eyes closed. A cool breeze snuck up on us. I shivered and looked over at Salim. He leaned against the doorframe and crossed his arms with his wet kurta-set clinging to his muscles. I watched him, watching Kushi.

I was sure he wanted to join her, but he probably knew that it would have ruined this moment. He watched his potential fiance dance in the rain, her saree hugging against her figure.

She took her shawl off her head and let her hair loose. I refused to ponder upon what Salim was thinking or, rather, imagining at that moment. Meanwhile, Kushi had no idea that she was being watched.

"Ahem," I pretended to clear my throat to get his attention. It didn't work, so I did it two more times, louder each time before he turned around and looked at me as if awoken from a dream.

"Sorry. That was inappropriate," he said, referring to his staring session.

"The part where you had a difficult time lowering your gaze?" I had to say it. I grinned.

He frowned as his body stiffened up. "Thank you for chaperoning." With that, he went back downstairs. I stayed behind, wondering when my cousin would wake up from her trance. Rain, I admit, was magical and as much as I wanted to join Kushi's dance, there was something holding me back. She just looked elated and I didn't want to mess that up for her. I smiled for the first time that day, remembering a quote by the legendary Muslim poet Rumi, "Raise your words, not your voice; it is rain that grows flowers, not thunder." I watched my cousin bloom before my eyes, but I wasn't sure what held her hand in the rain. *Perhaps, it was the whispers of coconut palms flying with the wind, sending her their prayers?*

When Kushi came back inside, I had a towel ready for her. I had run downstairs to grab one when I noticed she wasn't going to come back inside for a while.

"What happened?" I asked her.

"I was just trying to think."

"About what exactly?"

"My options."

"Well, I am happy that you realize you have more than one option."

Then, we went into her bedroom, where I helped take the pins off her saree and handed her a simple cotton salwar kameez.

During that moment, there was just silence, but of course, my head was exploding with questions that needed to be answered.

We sat down on her bed, Kushi's hair still wet as she held onto her blow dryer, powered off. I was still in my fancy salwar kameez, which I desperately wanted to change out of, but firstly, I needed to know: "What options?"

"If I seek help from Wings BD, I will risk losing my family or putting them at risk as Josh would still be out there; not everyone gets caught, Asha. Some guys get away with their crimes, while we live with the consequences forever."

"Then, what other option is there?" I asked her.

"If I refuse Josh, I might as well dig up my own grave now...perhaps, my parents' graves too."

"Stop thinking like that!" I withheld the sudden urge to slap her.

I didn't understand. Rain was supposed to empower her. She had been smiling in it!

"It's true."

"Please, just stop saying stuff like that. Why don't you just hear what Wings BD has to say about your situation? There's no harm in talking about it; they have experience in these kinds of things," I said.

"I know. I understand, but Salim doesn't seem all that bad."

"Oh, please, you're telling me you're going to marry some guy who's not 'all that bad?!' You spent a mere few minutes with him and you've already decided he's the 'one?!'" I couldn't help but fold my arms and roll my eyes at this.

"Why must you raise your voice?"

Trying to follow Rumi's advice on raising my words and not my voice in this situation had failed.

"I'm sorry, but I don't accept this."

"This marriage offer is not YOURS to accept!" She stood up with her fists and teeth clenched.

It was obvious that she had already made up her mind.

It was obvious that trying to convince her of anything otherwise would be like attempting to pull a banyan tree, roots and all, out of the earth with my bare hands.

"I'm sorry," I helplessly dragged out.

Just then, Khala walked in.

"Where have you two been? Kushi, you've changed already? They wanted to see you one last time before they left. His mother wanted to give you the ring."

"Ring? What ring?" She asked, alarmed.

"This ring," Khala opened up a little red box to reveal an intricate golden band. Kushi frowned at it.

Amma said, "It's not an official engagement ring, but it's a *promise* ring that is offered to us by the potential groom. It means he's interested in you. You must have made quite the impression, Kushi. But you should know that if you have any doubts about Salim, we can return the ring, and the groom's family will bear no hard feelings against you nor us."

Whew, it's a good thing that Kushi didn't go downstairs, then. She would have felt pressured into accepting the ring in front of everyone as if it were an *official* promise.

At least now, she could say, "No." This was her last chance and I prayed she would take it.

Kushi stared at the ring in silence for a moment. She was either thinking about accepting it or thinking of a way out of accepting it. How could she be thinking about it at all?! *N-O, NO. Two letters. One word. Simple, right? Take your chance, Sis! While you're at it, splurge all the details about Josh and you! Tell them about what's really happening! That you're being stalked, harassed, threatened....*

"Yes, okay," she said, stretching out her left hand, thereby offering her mother the honor of placing Salim's golden promise ring on her finger. I could not bear to watch, so I stomped out of her bedroom.

"What's wrong with Asha, Joyti?" Khala asked. "She should be congratulating her cousin; instead, she rudely leaves before witnessing such a big moment? You really need to teach your daughter some manners."

I imagined it upset Khala to see her daughter in tears, so she blamed it on my leaving, that somehow I was responsible for her sadness. What she barely noticed was that her daughter had been hurting for a very long time before I even met her. While Amma and I understood how overwhelming the circumstances were for Kushi, Khala *chose* to stay blind. *How could a mother not see her daughter...really, truly SEE her?*

That night, while everyone else was asleep, I could not. I tried counting numbers and gave up at 300. I recited as many prayers as I had memorized from the Quran. I put my hands together and prayed for Allah to save my cousin. Upon covering my face with my hands, I heard a scream. It sounded like it was Kushi. I ran to her bedroom to see her, in her bed, under her covers. She was talking in her sleep: "No, please don't, please don't do this to me, please! Please don't, please, please, please, I'm begging you, please!"

I grabbed her by the arms and shook her awake. "It's okay, it's okay, everything is okay. It's me, Asha. It's just me."

She wrapped her arms around me, buried her face into my neck and sobbed like a little girl. *She was a little girl.* The thought of Kushi having suffered sleep deprivation due to nightmares of Josh took me back to the moment when Victor Frankenstein refused to create a mate for the monster he had already awakened. He knew the consequences would be grave, but he felt the right or *just* thing to do was to never again create potentially-murderous creatures: *I was alone; none were near me to dissipate the gloom and relieve me from the sickening oppression of the most terrible reveries.... but I was overcome by the sensation of helplessness, so often felt in frightful dreams....*

I guessed that even if Kushi was not alone, she felt alone. That night, she cried herself back to sleep on my shoulder as I said a prayer and rubbed her head. Although it lasted just a few minutes, it felt like hours. My shoulders and neck ached from the strain of holding her up. But, I could care less about that. Even though I was still infuriated with Kushi for having accepted Salim's promise ring, I kissed her on the cheek and whispered, "Good night, Sis."

CHAPTER 9

THE DRESS

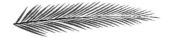

Kushi sat still, a member of the audience at a circus performance. There was a colorful assortment of fabrics performing acrobatics in the air; materials varied from rich silk and ornate brocade to wavy jacquard and soft chiffons.

"What do you think of this dress?" Khala pointed to one that landed on Kushi's lap.

"Or this one?" Amma pointed to another one that landed on Kushi's lap.

Kushi looked indifferent.

"I like it," Kushi robotically replied without looking at them properly.

"*Which* one do you like?" Khala asked.

"Point to it," I said, guessing it was harder for her to speak when reality, in the form of fabric, smacked her across the face before striking her lap.

She pointed to the light gray jacquard *lehenga* set, a top with matching skirt and shawl, gorgeously intricate with silver threadwork and crystals.

"Excellent choice for an engagement outfit!" The man with the thick mustache across the counter said.

We were shopping for Kushi's and Salim's engagement party. The date had been set not long after her ultimatum date from Josh.

Things were moving as quickly as a golden eagle, flying down to grab its prey with its sharp talons. Kushi had been diminished to prey in more ways than one.

Yet, she had on a bright pink tunic that made her glow even though she had lost her smile days ago. It seemed that the closer we got to the date when she would give Josh her answer to his proposal, the more difficult it was getting by the milliseconds, seconds, minutes and hours to dig the *real* Kushi out of the sand dune. I felt her slipping through my fingers again, but I knew she was there, somewhere. I just needed to reach for her hand and pull her out. *But how?*

I also wore a tunic, except mine was light pink. Looking into the mirror in one of the fitting rooms, I tied my frizzy hair up in a messy bun. I wasn't sure if the heat was *real* or if I was just feeling it from the inside. My neck was sweaty, though. Meanwhile, my cousin looked bewildered, slowly moving about the room as if she were in a dream or, rather, a nightmare. I so badly wanted to take her by the shoulders and shake her awake just as I did the night of the "promise" ring when she had been talking...screaming in her sleep! Instead, I managed to contain my rage and calmly walked toward her. I held her hand until our eyes met. I wondered if the whole sister-to-sister telepathic power truly existed. Just in case it did, I sent a message through my thoughts: *You can survive this; you are brave, but all heroes need their sidekicks; let me and Wings BD be yours.* She smiled at me before walking over to look at jewelry for her engagement outfit. Either she hadn't gotten my telepathic message, or she chose to ignore it. Something inside of me said that she had heard everything completely, but she had given up just as completely.

I lost myself within the circus of my own mind, silently watching from a distance. Kushi looked at twenty engagement outfits, trying on half of them and finally choosing one. *And now, for the accessories, shoes and matching clutch....* Every dress she tried on in the fitting room made her look splendid, even if she hadn't been feeling like it on the inside. We had been inside Zamila's parents' store for about an hour. Kushi and I weren't exactly on speaking terms since she had accepted the promise ring. I helplessly hoped that she would seek help from Wings BD.

A familiar voice called out to Kushi. "Kushi?! I came as soon as I heard you were here!" Zamila, wearing a flowery salwar kameez, hugged Kushi, but the hug was not returned.

Kushi struggled to put her arms around her. Either she had decided to deliberately push all of us away, to protect us in her own twisted way, or she had just forgotten what it felt like to be loved, the way one *should* be loved...without the psychological, emotional or physical torture.

"Where have you been?" Zamila yelled. "I haven't heard from you in so long! I even went to your house, but Abdul and Zulekha said you went to your nanabari."

282

Khala and Amma were too busy looking at jewelry to hear this conversation.

"I've been meaning to call you back," Kushi said.

"Why didn't you?" Zamila put her bag down on the chair, refusing to greet me. I had the feeling she purposefully ignored me, as if *I* were responsible for keeping Kushi away from her.

"I've been busy...." Kushi dragged out of herself. "Yeah, she's been busy...getting engaged!" I chimed in, failing to sedate my infuriated tone.

"What?!" Zamila finally spoke to me upon the realization that I was not the one keeping her best friend busy.

She looked at Kushi's hand for confirmation and noticed the promise ring. She hesitantly asked, "You're not engaged to *him*, are you?" By "him," she meant Josh.

Kushi shook her head.

"She still has four days left to give him her answer," I clarified.

"Then, why an engagement ring?"

"I'm engaged to someone else."

"Who is he?"

"A complete stranger," I harshly replied on my cousin's behalf.

Calm yourself down, Asha! Ganging up on your cousin, whom you call "Sis" won't make the situation any better!

"I guess Salim and I are still getting to know one another," Kushi added.

"It's more like you *barely* know each other and yet, here we are, looking for *the* dress."

"An engagement dress," she replied defensively. "Not a bridal one."

As if there was a difference at this point!

"Is this what you really want?" Zamila asked.

Of course it isn't! If you can't see it, don't call yourself anything close to a friend!

Kushi fiddled around with her ring while nodding her head.

"I don't believe it," Zamila said.

Yes! Finally! An ally!

"This was your plan all along.... You're finally seeing it through, aren't you?" Zamila pushed her curly curls behind her ears to see more clearly what was before her.

"What are you talking about?" I asked. "Planned what all along...to get married? Is that why you were looking at bridal outfits on the first day you brought me to the bazaar?" I looked at Kushi, who refused to meet my eyes with hers.

"Do you remember we talked about it and you decided *not* to see it through? What changed?" Zamila asked, holding Kushi's hands.

"Asha took me to a non-profit that helps girls like me. There were girls who had survived attacks...abuse of every kind and...there were also girls who had escaped, but in the process, lost contact with their families and...whatever 'normal' they had left in their lives."

I was slightly offended...no, actually, I was extremely offended that Kushi hadn't shared her thoughts about Wings BD with *me*. We were back to where we started: her calling me "Sis" but not really treating me like one. Meanwhile, she told Zamila the exact thing that I needed to hear from her these past few days. I could have guided her! I felt...betrayed, to say the least.

"Why didn't you say something?" I finally got up the nerve to ask.

"You were so mad at me that day when Salim and his family visited; I wasn't sure how to approach you after that."

I walked closer to her, put my hand on her shoulder and said, "I'm sorry. I guess I didn't make it easy on you."

"It's okay. I know you care about me, but the fact is that I need to get married now, or he'll never leave me alone."

Zamila said, "Did you ever think that if you reject Josh's marriage proposal, it'll be just as risky as him hearing about your engagement to another man from someone else?"

"Of course, I've considered it. But it's a risk I am willing to take."

"Every hero needs a sidekick; we're here for you," I said.

Kushi scoffed. "Hero? There's no hero or heroine in this story. There's only a predator and a prey. I'm just pleading with Allah that it won't, but it most probably *will*... end only *one* way."

"At what cost, Kushi?" Zamila asked. "You're losing yourself...."

"You've already lost yourself!" I abruptly said. "You can't expect us to dig you out of the hole you've buried yourself in without you letting us in with you first."

All three of us heard the dreaded motorcycle sound as it got parked outside of the shop. We ran to the window and looked down to see Josh removing his helmet. He then took out his phone and seemed to be sending a message to someone. Kushi's phone bleeped. She read out loud, "Heard you're shopping for a wedding dress. We should talk about that. I'll see you soon." He was just about to look up in our direction when we immediately ducked and distanced ourselves from the window, out of his sight.

"What should I do?" Kushi asked. This was the moment I had been waiting for, the moment she would open up to me enough to ask me for guidance. I took it by its wings and flew with it.

"Don't message back yet. We need to find another way out of here. Zamila, is there an emergency exit to the shop?"

"Do we really need to do this? He won't approach me in front of our moms, anyway," Kushi said.

I replied, "He approached us at your neighbor's wedding in front of everyone!"

"She's right," Zamila said. "I know another way out. We just need to get your moms to go along with it."

Khala and Amma showed Kushi a silver jewelry set for approval. As soon as she approved it, Zamila said, "Aunty, we're closing down a little early today, so our main door is locked at the moment. I will show you another way out. Abba, I'll be right back. I am just walking them out."

Her father nodded as we exited.

As we were on our way home in the car, Kushi held my hand as tightly as she did on the night we returned home from Srisha's and Ruhul's wedding.

"Volunteer with me tomorrow," I pleaded.

"I could barely stomach the last time we *volunteered*.

"This time will be different. You won't need to go into those sessions. You can do something else."

"Like what?"

"Serve food, maybe…I don't know? I'm sure there is something that won't require too much uncomfortable conversation." I kept my pleading eyes fixed on her, but she seemed unmoved. Who could blame her? It's a shelter, a hub for uncomfortable conversation! "I could really use the volunteer hours to get into the University of my choice, please, please help me, Sis."

"Maybe," she replied with a smile and a newfound hope grew its roots within me.

That night, I sat at the edge of my bed with *Frankenstein* begging me to read it. I just stared at the book, wondering…I loved reading Gothic literature; they were thrilling and adventurous! However, I also knew that reading *Frankenstein* at bedtime was basically inviting monsters into my sleeping brain, thereby causing nightmares. The truth was, however hazardous opening up the book could be, reading or writing were my lullabies. I had two choices: 1. Write another blog entry, however uninspired by the day's events or 2. Read myself into slumber even if the book was a haunting and tragic tale. After a few minutes of staring at *Frankenstein,* I read this:

> *We rest; a dream has power to poison sleep. We rise; one wand'ring thought pollutes the day. We feel, conceive, or reason; laugh or weep, Embrace fond woe, or cast our cares away; It is the same: for, be it joy or sorrow, The path of its*

departure still is free. Man's yesterday may ne'er be like his

morrow; Nought may endure but mutability!

I remembered reading those lines back in my Bronx bedroom and not understanding the words "nought" or "mutability," so I looked them up. I had penciled in notes about how change (mutability) was inevitable, but it was also the only constant or unchanging thing about life.

If Mary Shelley were alive, I would certainly have emailed her, asking her for guidance regarding my cousin's morbid circumstances. I imagined she would have replied to my email with something related to the word " mutability:" *Change is inevitable, uncontrollable and the only thing that is certain in life, but we do have control over how we bear it.* And I would have replied back: *In that case, Kushi and I will bear it or, rather, handle it fearlessly.* The newfound hope that had begun growing its roots within me, veined its way deeper and deeper until it rocked me to sleep.

CHAPTER 10

THE WAKE-UP CALL

Standing in front of Wings BD, hope growing its leaves around me, I suddenly got a flashback of a high school moment. Rumor had it that the valedictorian, at the time, had been forced into an arranged marriage in India and settled down there. Our class, as a result, was extra chaotic that day. Our AP English teacher was the only one that could grab our attention and did so by slamming a stack of books onto his desk as loudly as he could. Then, he recited a quote by Khalil Gibran, a Lebanese-American published author, poet and philosopher from the early 20th century: "If you reveal your secrets to the wind, you should not blame the wind for revealing them to the trees."

At present, my cousin had entrusted me with her secret, but I wondered if I should become wind and bring that secret to the coconut trees. Technically, I already had when I asked the coconut palms at nanabari for their advice. Still, no matter how inspiring nature had been, its force had not influenced my cousin enough to seek help.

A breeze played with our hair and the hems of our tunics. I looked over at Kushi and wondered if it would rain and whether or not we should consider that rain as a blessing for us on that day, the day that my cousin had agreed to join me on a venture that could possibly change our lives forever.

With that thought, I felt a shoulder slam against mine. If we were in New York City, people accidentally brushed or slammed against shoulders while walking on concrete sidewalks at such a speed that there was never time to stop and apologize for it. But this was not New York City. This was Sylhet and no matter how overpopulated the city had been, I had yet to brush shoulders with anyone. Until that dreaded day.

Kushi heard me yelp and asked, "Are you okay?"

"Yeah…. What's the big fuss?" I referred to the two women running havoc, one in a police uniform and the other in a simple salwar kameez.

"There's Onthara, the officer, and Ishitha, the counselor!" Kushi said.

"Let's ask what's going on," I said.

We walked over to Ohthara, who was listening to some static communication on the police radio.

"Her name is Zamila, dog attack," Othara said to Ishitha just as we reached them to figure out what was happening.

"What did you just say?" Kushi asked. Her eyes seemed as wide as a cave, becoming cloudy from the smoke of rocks colliding in and blocking the exit of her mind. I wanted to dive in and pull her out, but it was too late. They had repeated the name, *Zamila,* and she nearly fell before I caught her.

"Maybe, it's not *our* Zamila," I said to Kushi.

"We need to find out. Can we go with you, please?"

Onthara was about to say something before Ishitha immediately said, "No. Impossible. Based on the prognosis from our last meeting together, you're not ready for this."

"Please, I'm begging you." Kushi's eyes flooded with tears and Onthara realized that the victim, awaiting their arrival to rescue her at the hospital, could very well be someone Kushi personally knew. Ishitha puffed out a long sigh.

"It's okay," Onthara said.

"But…" Ishitha attempted to defend her so-called prognosis again.

"Hop in," Onthara said, allowing us to get into the backseat of the police vehicle.

I just held Kushi's hand the entire ride. Her head lay on my shoulder, soaking the cloth that protected it. I didn't mind. I just prayed that the girl Wings BD was trying to save was not Kushi's best friend. No matter how sorry I felt for the girl who was lying in a hospital bed due to an attack that could very well have been maliciously intended, I still prayed it was not the vibrant personality of curls I had come to know and respect.

Onthara showed her badge before she entered the room. I looked at Kushi one last time and asked with my eyes, *Are you ready to go in?* Still holding my hand, she was the one that led *me* in. *How brave of her!* I thought to myself. *Not our Zamila,* I kept repeating in my head. Onthara had already begun interviewing a woman in a colorful saree. She appeared to be the patient's mother. In the midst of the interview, the woman ran up to Kushi, wrapped her arms around her, and sobbed into her neck until Kushi let go of my hand, wrapped her arms around her and sobbed into *her* neck. That was when I noticed a few locks of the patient's hair spread across the hospital bed pillow, her helpless body wrapped in bandages, her mind unconscious, but I imagined it was screaming from excruciating pain. And it finally hit me that the patient was, indeed, Zamila and the woman crying with Kushi, was Zamila's mother.

I caught myself by leaning over the footboard of her bed, *knowing* it was not just any accidental attack; rather, I firmly believed it was an intentional murder attempt by none other than Josh! He had used his dog as a weapon and the vicious attack must have been a warning sign for Kushi. He was probably telling her, *I will break your loved ones, thereby breaking your spirit before I ultimately break YOU!*

And all the while, I kept telling myself that we could bear this fearlessly, that we could survive this, that we were all in this together, Zamila, Kushi and I; all the while, not fully comprehending what this man was capable of doing until he actually *did* it; all the while, I thought we could save ourselves from his wrath when his wrath had already been so visible, yet I ignored it. I thought I could just guess how my cousin had been feeling and what she had been going through, but guessing is not truly knowing.

Had I been plain stupid? Was I just plain dumb? *AM I a complete idiot?* No matter how much I didn't want to admit it, no matter how much I wanted Kushi to chase the end of the rainbow like all girls should, I wondered whether or not I should just give up...admit defeat. Should I just accept that my cousin was forever stuck at the beginning of the rainbow and that I was stuck there with her, holding her hand and lying to her about how it was possible to get to the other side of it? Would she ever truly recognize her dreams, follow them to the end and discover a world beyond just marriage? Or was it best to begin this question with, "could she…" rather than "would she…?"

Kushi was by Zamila's bedside. Onthara and Ishitha decided to speak to the doctor and assess the circumstances. Watching Zamila's body, unmoving, her eyes shut, my deep-rooted hope was on its knees, begging for water and light.

Meanwhile, Kushi's phone bleeped. She couldn't get herself to pick it up and look at her messages, but I needed to know for certain what had happened... so I took her phone out of her satchel, which hung over the chair she was seated on. And there they were, Josh's words across the screen, "I hope our wedding night will be less dramatic than this." Instinctively, I ran out of the room and hysterically begged Onthara, "Help her! Please, please, you have to help her!"

She rubbed my shoulders, "Don't worry, Asha. We will help your friend as soon as she is recovered and we can get the full story on what *really* happened. Witnesses say that this wasn't just an accident; they saw the dog with its male owner. It was a witness that called the incident in. We will make sure to catch the guy who did this and everything will be okay."

"No, I don't mean Zamila. Of course, you should help her, but you need to help Kushi, too! She can't survive this...*him*, without your help."

Onthara sat me down on a chair in the waiting room. "Ishitha, get Asha a glass of water, please." After

Ishitha left, Onthara asked, "What are you talking about? What's going on with Kushi?"

I took off with the wind. In just a matter of minutes, I had broken my cousin's trust and disclosed *everything*. I told Onthara about how Kushi had met Josh. I told her about Josh's violent and controlling nature. I told her about his marriage proposal and how he had left scars on Kushi's wrists. I revealed Kushi's plan to escape his wrath by marrying another man, but it only incited his anger and that fury led us to the hospital, where Kushi's best friend lay in a hospital bed. I told her how Josh's obsession with Kushi was lethal, that it caused him to deliberately set his dog loose on her best friend as a warning sign to Kushi. Remembering my own nightmare from a few days back, I had to tell Onthara one more thing before I, myself, burst into tears: "That girl you see, in that hospital bed...that girl could have easily been *me*!" As if I had suddenly realized that fact, I repeated, "It could have been me. It could have been *me!*" I frantically swayed back and forth as Onthara held me. She whispered, "Shh...shh...it's okay. We'll take care of you, all three of you; everything will be alright."

For the first time, I finally understood how helpless...*hope*less my cousin had been feeling all along. The worst part was that I no longer believed we could survive this.

The leaves of my hope withered as my salty tears were not healthy enough to water it.

Just then, I felt a hand on my shoulder.

Kushi stood there with her puffy eyes and runny nose. Her hair was a mess.

Ishitha offered me water. I thanked her and drank it.

"Onthara...." Kushi began. "Have a seat, Dear. Try to calm down." Ishitha tried to take her hand, but Kushi snatched her hand back, screaming, "No! I can't! How can I sit down and relax when my best friend is hurt...and it's all because of me! It's all my fault! Go ahead and arrest me." She blubbered before falling to her knees on the floor. "It's all my fault. It's all my fault...." She repeated this over and over again, losing herself completely. Onthara, Ishitha and I helped Kushi back onto her feet and took her outside for some fresh air. She wouldn't stop saying it was her fault and nothing we said made her stop punishing herself by drowning herself in the tsunami of unjustified guilt. Ishitha sat down next to Kushi in the police car. Meanwhile, Onthara nudged me to follow her further away from it.

"Listen, Asha. I understand you're hurting, too, and this is all a shock to you. However, I know a way we can help Kushi."

"What is it?" I half-heartedly asked. I was exhausted from crying and then having to drag a girl much taller than I out of the hospital. I stared at the firy marigolds, waving at me from the roadside in the distance.

Onthara snapped her fingers in front of my face to regain my attention. As she explained to me her elaborate master plan and the many ways I could help, something I had wanted to do since I first found out about Josh. I just gave her a blank stare. It wasn't because I didn't want to believe her plan would work; rather, it was because I didn't believe her plan would work. "Of course, I would have to assess the risks involved and have backup ready." The only word I heard at that moment was "risks."

"I'll think about it," I replied.

"Think about what exactly?"

I shrugged my shoulders.

"Think about whether or not you want to help?"

"Oh no...I want to help, really, I do," I was trying to convince myself more than I was trying to convince

Onthara. "I just...I just don't know that I can, considering...the *risks* involved."

"I have to be honest with you. Anyway, you have until tomorrow to decide whether or not you *can* help."

Ishitha overheard some part of the conversation and said, "You have an entire organization and police on your side. You have to ask yourself, 'Are the risks worth taking when they can be managed and controlled? Are the risks worth taking when all this time, I thought I was completely alone, but now... I have an army behind me?' You need to think about Kushi and Zamila and ask yourself, 'Are the risks worth taking if the chances of winning are much higher than the chances of losing *this* time?' " That was the most sensible thing she had ever said to me, and I wondered if she, too, read Mary Shelley. I looked over my shoulder at Kushi, at her weakest point, and said, "Okay...I'm in!"

That night, I opened up my blog. I tried to think of a way to begin my blog post, but my heart wasn't in it. Just then, Amma walked in. "What are you writing?" She asked.

"Nothing, literally," I robotically replied.

She read my eyes, but instead of confronting me, she tried to cheer me up. "Your last blog post had me asking your Abba to bring me a box of tissues."

"Aw, really?" I giggled.

"Really. And, thank you." She put her arms around my shoulders.

"Amma, I should be the one thanking you!"

"And you *did*, in your post and in the most beautiful words."

She took a chair and sat down next to me at the desk. I stared at the blank draft and sighed. She sighed, too, and folded her hands on top of the table, patiently waiting for me to open up to her. And I did eventually: "I have an obsession with trying to find the beautiful behind all things ugly, especially when I write about them. Do you think that's wrong of me...dishonest?"

"I don't think you have an *obsession*. I think you are exemplary. You want to give people something to *hope* for and be happy about. It doesn't mean you're hiding the ugly *behind* the beautiful. You're just trying to find the beautiful *in* the ugly. And that, my dear, is a very noble thing to do."

"Now, *I'm* going to need a tissue box," I said.

"Aw, Shuna!" Amma hugged me before continuing. "I don't know what's going on with you or Kushi, but know that if and when you're ready to talk, I'm here, okay?"

I nodded. "I know." While knowing this and having *known* it all along, I still couldn't bring myself to tell my mother about the battlefield I had been walking on...about the guerilla warfare I would be embarking on.

Dinner was as quiet as a snowy day. I could almost see the breath vapor smoking out of our mouths. I shivered when I noticed Kushi's glum facial expressions as she noticed worry in her mother's eyes. *When a daughter could see "worry" in her mother's eyes, what does that say about their relationship?* I asked myself. Before I could venture any deeper into the thought, Khala slammed her drinking glass on the table.

"I can't do this anymore. We need to tell her," she said, not daring to look up at the person she was actually addressing.

"Joyti!" Khalu replied. "This isn't the time nor place."

"Will there ever be a right time, Nil?" This time, she looked him straight in the eyes. Amma and Abba, feeling awkward, met each other's eyes. Kushi and I looked at each other wide-eyed.

Fortunately for Zulekha and Abdul, they missed the tension of this staring contest.

"What's going on?" Kushi asked, her voice quivering.

Had Khala and Khalu figured out what was going on in our lives? Had they broken off Kushi's engagement as a result? Had they filed a complaint to the authorities? Had they threatened Josh and his family?

"Kushi…," Khalu began before Khala broke into tears and ran out of the dining room. "Your friend, Zamila…she's…she's in the hospital. She's been attacked by…."

"A dog? I know. I visited her today at the hospital," Kushi replied as she had rehearsed it.

Why did she admit this?

Khalu looked baffled. "Why didn't you say something?" He asked.

Kushi shrugged her shoulders.

"Khalu..." I began. "I think the visit was too painful for Kushi to talk about. It's all so fresh. I think she's still trying to process it." I hoped I wasn't being rude by interfering in their father-daughter dialogue.

Kushi rested her head on her hand and played around with the rice on her plate.

"I see," was all that Khalu could say.

I wasn't convinced he understood what I had meant. I wasn't sure if my words had offended him in any way as if to accuse him of not understanding his own daughter. I wasn't sure if, like meteorites, my words had traveled through the atmosphere at such a speed that they crashed through a rather significant moment in all of our lives.

Should I have just waited to hear Kushi's response? Should I have let Khalu go on nagging her about why she had been quiet about the whole incident? Should I have just...no...no...I care about Kushi too much, and what I did was, at the least, okay, if not right.

Khala still did not return to the dining room.

And there it was again, the snow and the breath vapor. I shivered.

Lying down in bed that night, my mind, my heart, and my body had invited worry, concern and anxiety into the room. On top of that, fear knocked on my door. I refused to let it in because otherwise, it would stop me from fighting alongside my cousin...*for* my cousin. Fear got angry and banged on my door. I shut my eyes, stuck my head under the blanket and covered my ears with my pillows. I said my prayers. Immediately afterward, I remembered Amma's comforting words, *"You're just trying to find the beautiful in the ugly. And that, my dear, is a very noble thing to do."* She had been right. My cousin represented and showed me so much of what was beautiful about Bangladesh and then, there was the ugly that lurked in the darkest of alleyways, waiting to pounce on her and consume her innocence, her dreams, her friends, her family, her *everything*...her *all*. Not anymore! I was going to help her get it *all* back. Fear surrendered. Worry, concern and anxiety rested. And I finally dozed off to sleep.

CHAPTER 11

THE STALKER

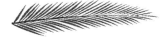

"Who is that?" Kushi asked, referring to the woman stepping outside of a police vehicle. She had on a simply-embroidered salwar kameez, chandelier earrings, *kajol* under her eyes, winged eyeliner and bright red lipstick. Her hair was a loose set of curls.

"She doesn't look like a criminal…." I replied, referring to the vehicle she had just stepped out of. "She's not even wearing handcuffs."

Kushi looked pensive for a moment before speaking.

"She's definitely not a police officer," Kushi replied.

"Then, why is she stepping out of a police vehicle and walking toward us?" I asked.

"Are we ready, girls?" The woman spoke to us and we immediately recognized her voice.

"Onthara?!" Kushi and I unanimously asked, gawking at her.

"Officer Onthara, at your service."

We didn't realize we were still staring until Onthara waved her hands in front of our faces.

Then, she looked down at her own salwar kameez and realized why we had been gaping at her.

"Oh! That's right...you've never seen me out-of-uniform before." She giggled.

"I'm undercover today disguised as basically...anybody. I could be anybody." The corners of her lips quivered as she smiled. I guessed she hadn't been sure whether or not it was appropriate to smile at all, considering the mission-at-hand. Regardless, I sensed Onthara longed for these kinds of missions, the kind where she caught the bad person while being any person. I looked over at Kushi, who hadn't uttered another word, before noticing a man closing in on Onthara.Hair slicked back, he had on a slim-fit blazer and a pair of jeans.

"Hello, I'm Officer Badar," he said.

"Officer Badar will be playing the role of my fiance."

"We are going to catch that dog and put him behind bars for good!" Officer Badar said.

"Catch the actual dog or its master, who happens to be the biggest dog of all?" I asked, half-smiling.

Meanwhile, Kushi just stared off into space.

My eyes fell upon the diamond ring on Onthara's

finger and I began to wonder if it was

all really just a part of the act. The way Onthara and Badar

were looking at one another so adoringly, it all seemed too

real to be just an act.

"Is that diamond ring real?" I asked her.

"Yes," she replied.

"Do you own it, or is it a borrowed prop?"

Onthara blushed.

"Are you two...?" I asked, adjusting my orna a bit.

Onthara met Badar's eyes and he gave her a firm

nod.

"We *are* really engaged, but we were assigned to

work on this mission together. It just...happened to be this

way."

I smiled inwardly and then I spoke.

"You don't have to explain," I said.

"No, it's okay," Badar chimed in. "When I heard how much this mission meant to Onthara, I just knew I had to get on board."

"So...you're not really undercover, then?" Kushi narrowed her eyes.

Why did she suddenly look so mad?

"We are out of uniform. Anyway, the rest of the team is already in their positions. Let's get going." With that, Onthara swiftly turned around and walked toward her vehicle.

As we followed closely behind, Kushi asked Badar, "Did you know before you proposed?"

"Did I know what?" He asked.

"...That Onthara is a divorcee?"

He snorted and looked off at a distance, at nothing in particular. Onthara ignored the comment. I noticed her hands by her side, forming fists.

"I guess you did, then," Kushi said, folding her arms together.

I thought that was the end of that, but for some reason, she couldn't let it go.

"So, this is the first time I see a divorcee moving forward and getting engaged while the husband-to-be knows all about her history."

"Congratulations, by the way, on your engagement!" I quickly said, hoping my words snapped the tension in the car.

"Thank you," Onthara replied with a genuine smile.

Kushi smirked.

As she drove, Onthara got a glimpse of Kushi through the rearview mirror. Badar sat in the front passenger seat beside his fiance.

"Kushi," Onthara began, poised. "You're a girl...*ahem*, a woman who is being stalked. Perhaps you can be defined as 'stalked,' 'victimized,' your *entire* life? Or, maybe, once having survived the circumstances as I am confident you will, you would prefer to be called strong rather than stalked, '*valiant*' rather than victimized? There is life beyond this, Kushi; you just have to live it."

I concluded that Kushi wasn't mad at anybody; rather, she was envious of Onthara, who had reminded us that the freedom to define ourselves was within our grasp; we just needed to grab it in order to have it. In a way, that's what we were trying to do that day.

I rubbed my cousin's shoulders. "You got this!" I whispered to her. She grinned.

Once we arrived at the bazaar, Onthara guided us, with her eyes, toward our location.

As we began walking, we turned around to see Onthara and Badar heading toward a restaurant across the street.

Kushi and I had our gear on; simple kurtis, jeans and running shoes. Kushi had on a little extra gear...a hidden wire to record our conversation with Josh if and when he arrived. Like Onthara had said to us before, *He knows where you are at all times; he has eyes and ears everywhere; he will find you.* We suggested that Kushi contact him and lure him to the location, but Onthara said it would seem less suspicious not to. After all, police also had eyes and ears everywhere and they had been expecting Josh to show up to hear Kushi's answer to his marriage proposal.

The staircase that led up to Zamila's parents' shop suddenly looked infinite. We wanted to climb it but couldn't get ourselves to do it.

"Remind me why we're here again?" Kushi asked me.

Up until that point, I hadn't thought about how emotional this must have been for my cousin, going into the very shop of her best friend, who was lying in a hospital bed. It was like grabbing trauma by the shoulders and looking it straight in the eyes.

"I know this is difficult for you." I held her hand. "I'm here, Sis. Officer Onthara said that we are here because of *patterns*. Stalkers, like most criminals, have patterns and habits. This is a place Josh knows you feel some connection to. He's expecting you to return to it."

"Did Onthara make you memorize a script or something?" Kushi asked, holding tightly onto the railing to the staircase as if she might fall at the slightest distraction.

Yes, Officer Onthara from Wings BD had made me memorize a script...kind of, sort of. But I couldn't tell Kushi that. It was information that could make her even more trepidatious than she had already been. All I knew was that we had a set plan and I was praying it went accordingly. The Wings BD counselor, Ishitha, helped me prepare for this day and advised me not to bombard Kushi with the details. I kept thinking back to when I first met Ishitha and how infuriated I was with her, believing she was completely useless at her job.

Then, I thought back to the moment I had given up all hope, standing outside of the hospital, having just visited Zamila, and wanting so desperately to help but thinking that I couldn't. It was a moment where Ishitha showed that she was actually *great* at her job. I thought back to what she had said to me: "You have an entire organization and police on your side. You have to ask yourself, 'Are the risks worth taking when they can be managed and controlled?

Are the risks worth taking when all this time, I thought I was completely alone, but now... I have an army behind me?' You need to think about Kushi and Zamila and ask yourself, 'Are the risks worth taking if the chances of winning are much higher than the chances of losing *this* time?"'

After having gone over our mission, "Stalk the Stalker," Onthara paused and looked at Kushi and me in such a way that I figured she wanted us to say something.

But we remained quiet.

I wasn't sure what, though.

"Why do we have an army going against one man?" Kushi had finally asked.

Now, of all the stupid things she could have asked as if she were defending Josh as if he deserved any kind of empathy whatsoever!

"What makes you so certain he is working alone?" Onthara had asked.

"What makes you so certain he isn't?" Kushi replied.

Now, of all the stupid things she could have asked! I repeated in my head, shaking it in sheer disappointment.

"How else does he know about your whereabouts? How else does he show up out of nowhere with impeccable timing? Do you *always* tell him where you are and when you're going there?" Onthara asked.

Kushi shook her head. I wanted to believe that she wasn't being stupid, that maybe she was just making sure Onthara knew what she was doing.

"Actually..." I began because now, of all the stupid things I could have asked, I did it anyway. "You've screenshotted all of the text messages that Kushi and Josh have exchanged. You have photographs and video footage that I have taken of their encounter with one another. You have security footage from when Zamila was attacked. You even have witnesses and if they're not willing to give a statement, then I am more than ready to do it! So... why stalk the stalker when you have enough evidence to handcuff the guy and throw him into jail at this very moment?"

Perhaps, I was also making sure Onthara knew what she was doing.

She replied, "Text messages can easily be twisted into Kushi seducing Josh or being in a secret relationship with him all along. The photographs and videos could have been misleading. The camera footage of the dog attack does not fully determine Josh's identity. Witnesses do not always want to give *official* statements because they fear *also* becoming victims or they fear their names...*ahem*, their reputations will be tarnished. And Shuna, as much as you are ready to give that official statement, you're Kushi's cousin and *that* relation will deter any credibility you have as a reliable witness. And these are all of the things that any lawful official or advocate will throw at you before Josh can ever be handcuffed and thrown into jail."

"Got it," I replied, pushing my chair back to get up. I looked around Onthara's office and noticed different

SECRETS IN THE WIND

certificates framed on the walls, but no family photographs. Had she also lost her family in the process of divorcing her abuser and completing her police academy course? Or did she just want to protect them, as her job required dangerous encounters with criminals?

"Any more questions, anyone?" She looked around... I shook my head.

"Yes, one last question from me," Kushi said. "How can we tell your people apart from Josh's people when we are being followed and watched?"

"Our people will be the least suspicious ones, among a crowd, undercover in our different roles.

You won't even know who we are. And you shouldn't let anyone know what your true intentions are. Just keep living your life and we will observe." Kushi solemnly got up from her chair. Onthara put her hand on hers. Their eyes met and she said, "Kushi, we *will* win this fight. You will be free of him."

On our way out, Ishitha pulled me aside and whispered into my ear, "We will go over the different scenarios later." She winked at me, which meant I should keep that part of our meeting clandestine from Kushi.

I found myself standing outside of the shop door while Kushi stood behind me.

"Excuse me," a customer said on her way out. We had to lean back against the railing to let her exit downstairs.

What were we waiting for?

"Isn't this going to put Zamila's parents and her in more danger?" Kushi whispered to me.

"I honestly didn't think of that." The truth was that I only thought of saving my cousin, getting revenge for

Zamila and putting Josh behind bars. There would be risks and risks were worth taking with an army behind us, I kept telling myself.

We walked into the shop, but Zamila's parents were nowhere to be found. They had other employees working for them that day...employees that did not recognize us. We walked around, still admiring the rich fabrics of our culture. This was one thing I loved so much about Bangladesh, its vibrancy. For once, in playing pretend, I lost myself in a world where things seemed normal, where there was just my cousin and I nonchalantly shopping on a girls' day out.

Things looked peaceful for a moment because just as quickly as I lost myself, it was that quickly that I lost my cousin. She wasn't behind me or near me; she wasn't in the shop at all. I ran outside to see her hyperventilating on the staircase.

"What's wrong? You need some water?" I pulled a bottle out of my bag and handed it to her.

She gulped it down. I brushed her hair away from the sweat beads forming on her forehead. I met her eyes.

"Kushi?"

"Yes, Asha?"

She looked like she was about to pass out. I rubbed her shoulders.

"You're going to be fine," I whispered. What I really wanted to say was, *You need to stop being so afraid; you're going to give us away like this. I know it's not easy, but you have to try*.... I figured that would have sounded too insensitive. She nodded and I mustered up another idea to calm her nerves: "Pretend...pretend I've just come from America and you're going to show me around; pretend you've never met

330

Josh; you have to put yourself in that mindset. Think about a time when you felt the happiest with Zamila...with your parents?" A light breeze brushed against my frizzy hair and I could hear something whisper into my ear. *Were the coconut palms trying to tell me something? Was the red sun about to set soon? Was the wind spreading secrets past us?* I wished I could hear them clearly enough at that moment, but I was confident that secrets were meant to be revealed at one point or another.

"Well, one time, Zamila and I visited her grandparents' home in the village and we watched the sunset while sipping on coconut water directly from coconuts; Oh, and I loved dancing in the rain with you at nanabari! It was so much fun!" Kushi smiled widely and looked off into a distance where she could visualize it all. "Another time, Abba took me to his office once; he sat me down at his desk and took a photograph of me. He told me that someday, I might be sitting at a desk chair in my own office…" Just then, her smile disappeared and she lowered her gaze toward the ground.

"The dream is still real!" I repeated, "The dream is still real!"

She mumbled, "And Amma bought me my first English book. It was a workbook, but it was the first time I began to fall in love with the language. She spent every day teaching me after teaching her own class."

"The dream was always there, wasn't it? It still is…remember that it still is. Think of those moments that will keep your chin up as we descend."

We both adjusted our ornas and flung them over our shoulders, pretending to be as confident as ever. Kushi looked like she was standing up a little straighter. We reached a point where we could still spot Onthara and Badar dining at a restaurant across the street. They noticed us staring but ignored us. *They should win an Emmy or Oscar for this*, I thought to myself.

"They look so happy together, don't they, Asha?" *Kushi asked me.*

I nodded before our vision became blurred by a familiar face. He batted his long eyelashes in awe of my cousin's beauty.

"Salim?" Kushi began. "What are you doing here?"

How did I miss this? I was as alert as a deer and still didn't see this one coming!

Salim replied with a lot of ohs and ums. Maybe he was flabbergasted by Kushi's beauty? Or he ran into us coincidentally and it took him by surprise? Or maybe *he* was stalking us and not expecting to get caught?

"Well?" I asked. "Answer her! What are you doing here?!" Salim narrowed his eyes at me. He probably still held onto a grudge against me for interrupting his trance when he watched my cousin dance in the rain on her rooftop.

"Um...I was actually going to see what dress you picked out so that I could match my sherwani with it."

"Oh…." Kushi replied.

"Oh…." I replied, joining Salim's chorus of ohs and ums, searching the air for explanations. *Did we have to explain ourselves to him?*

He rubbed his arms up and down as if a chill snuck up on him. "It was Amma's idea!" He said defensively as if it being his own idea would have been considered wrong.

"It's okay," Kushi replied. "It's...sweet."

Did she really mean that, or was she just playing along? Was she actually planning on going through with the engagement or was she waiting for the right moment to tell him it's off?

I wanted to tell him to wipe that goofy smile off his face, but before I could think any further, a motorcycle zoomed in. It came to a sudden halt and Josh took off his helmet. He leaned against the bike, looked directly at Kushi and said, "Shall we set the date today?"

"That's it?!" I said.

"That's your grand gesture? That's how you propose to the love of your life? Don't you even want to hear her say 'Yes' before you assume it is a yes?"

OMG Asha, where is all this coming from?!

He snorted and waved his hand as if shooing away mosquitoes.

"Too *American* for me."

"I don't even get any flowers?" Kushi asked with the same grace I had noticed in her at our first meeting.

"Wait a minute. Who is this guy, Kushi?" Salim asked.

"Yeah, Kushi. Tell him who I am," Josh said.

Kushi stiffened as Salim waited for her to answer.

"Tell him about our relationship," Josh continued. He folded his arms in a calm manner.

"Relationship?!" Salim asked. "What's he talking about? Why aren't you saying anything?" Then, he turned toward me and asked, "What happened to you? Are you so buried beneath your own words now that you can't put together a sentence?"

"You speak English very well," I finally said.

"Oh well, I would thank you if you weren't trying to distract me from the main point here!" Salim said. Then, he asked Kushi, "Who is this guy?"

"Ay!" Josh got so close that his nose almost touched Salim's. His glare was painful enough for Salim to take a few steps backward. "Be careful who you call THIS guy! I'm THE guy," Josh replied. He then poked Salim's chest. "You got that, *foa*?" The word "foa" was Bengali for "boy" in the Sylheti dialect. With that, Josh's eyes grew bloodshot red and I swore I saw a volcano explode within them. And Salim's eyes were a mix of fear and sheer disappointment. He just looked down at his sandals, shook his head and escaped the scene, quite possibly with his life. In Salim's eyes, Kushi had been nothing but a cheater and he was probably going to tell his mother all about his encounter with Kushi's secret lover.

Josh analyzed Kushi with curious eyes. "Since when do you ask for things from me? Flowers?!" He then eyed me while still speaking to Kushi, "You've never made commands before; something has changed in you." As he neared us, I got the inclination that he despised bold women. He probably sensed he was losing control.

Only Kushi and I knew that he would, indeed, lose control of her. "I see you're at your favorite shop," he said stating the obvious. "You know me so well," Kushi replied, almost flirtatiously.

"I didn't think you'd return after...nevermind."

I saw my cousin's lips shut tighter and her nose flaring.

"You do know me *very* well, but you're not the only one. Others know me well too. So, technically, just knowing me well enough doesn't make me the one for you."

You tell 'em, girl!

He was now closer to her...to *us* that even I could feel his breath blowing from a distance.

"Forget the flowers," he said. "Choose, instead, the dress, the matching jewelry, the matching shoes, the matching purse. It's all on me."

The gall!

I was now shoulder-to-shoulder with my cousin. He shot me a repulsed look.

Picking a bundle of her hair up in his hands, he said to Kushi, "Maybe, you could put your hair up on the big day?" I heard my cousin whimper as Josh was pulling her hair so hard that she struggled to keep her head straight.

Passersby looked on and did nothing. Maybe, they were too scared themselves; maybe, they just didn't care to get involved; maybe, they thought this was a domestic issue between husband –and wife or brother –and sister. Nevertheless, I reminded myself that we didn't need them; we had enough people on our side; we had Wings BD and the police. I decided that I was going to do something.

"Let go of her," I demanded.

He glared at me and pulled harder.

"I said, let go of her!" I desperately searched over his shoulder to see that Onthara and Badar were no longer inside the restaurant. I prayed they were on their way to us. After all, Kushi had been wired up so that they could hear and record everything and come to our rescue in the nick of time. "Say something," I encouraged Kushi. "Tell him how you really feel about him, Kushi! Tell him what you really think about him!"

"Let go of my hair, Josh! You're hurting me!" She pleaded. Just as we had planned, she shouted her answer loudly and clearly enough. "I don't want to marry you; I will *not* marry you...EVER. I never wanted to!"

"Why are you forcing yourself onto a girl who doesn't even want you?!" I yelled.

"What did you say, you little...." And Josh muttered what I gathered was a bunch of swear words in the Bengali language, words I had never heard before.

Suddenly, his enraged rant turned into the scream of a man who was in excruciating pain. Officer Badar had twisted Josh's arms around and handcuffed the son-of-a-bunch of swear words I uttered in English...in my head. It took Josh a few seconds to realize what was happening. The rivers of red in his eyes had receded. The corners of his growling mouth began shaking. His eyebrows, which were curved inward, were now curved upward. He was scared...helpless. We no longer felt scared or helpless.

Kushi looked exhausted. She backed up and sat down on the staircase of the shop again as we watched the scene. Suddenly, passersby cared enough to take out their phones to record the event.

A news reporter in a white shirt and gray pants appeared before us, his cameraman following closely behind. It was as if they were waiting around for the arrest to happen.

They focused their camera on Josh and tried but failed to interview the arresting officers, Onthara and Badar.

"You girls, go home to your families," Onthara said. "Listen, Onthara, I'm sorry," Kushi whispered, regarding her reaction to Onthara's engagement on the car ride over.

"No worries at all, Dear. You're safe now. Take care." She nodded toward someone waiting for us in the distance. It was Ishitha, who had been undercover in a baggy saree as a bangles saleswoman. We hadn't even noticed her among the crowd. Suddenly, there were others rising up and joining the task force, including a woman who had been sipping chai near a kiosk, a man who had been reading a newspaper and a man who had been getting his beard trimmed at the local barber.

These were just a few members of our army! Some of them were even appointed for crowd control. Ishitha was there to escort us home.

The news reporter badgered us for comments as we made our way into a car. As we drove off, I noticed Salim speaking into his phone in the distance. He waved his hands up and down in a rage. He was probably telling his mother about our unfortunate encounter.

Inside the car, I finally got a better look at my cousin, who rubbed her scalp. "Are you okay?" I asked.. *Stupid question, Asha!* "What can I do?" *Much better!*

"I have a feeling the ache will go away soon. Right now, I'm just replaying what happened over and over again in my head."

"Me too."

"Girls, you're safe now," Ishitha said.

We gave her a blank stare. Every time I blinked, I felt like I was waking up over and over again. I even rubbed my eyes as if that would make the blur disappear and a more translucent reality appear. Just then, I remembered a scene from *Frankenstein*: "*All was again silent, but his words rang in my ears. I burned with rage to pursue the murderer of my peace and precipitate him into the ocean. I walked up and down my room hastily and perturbed, while my imagination conjured up a thousand images to torment and sting me.*"

"Josh is off the streets," Ishitha said, shattering my thought of a thousand images.

Upon hearing those words, I noticed the foggy windows of the car clear up and the light of the red sun seep through enough for us to feel its arms cradle us.

"Josh is off the streets," Ishita repeated. "Everything is going to be okay. You don't have to worry about him bothering you anymore. This wasn't his first time."

"What if he gets back on the streets?" Kushi asked.

"Not this time. He won't," Ishitha said. "Trust me."

Kushi nodded. "Okay, but why do I feel like he's still out there?"

I hadn't said it, but I felt the same way.

Ishitha placed her hand on Kushi's. "It's because you've gotten used to life with him around and so much of it will stay with you...in your mind. Eventually, you'll let go...I know you will let go. It'll just take some time."

We were home, where our parents had been anxiously waiting for us. They had figured out that we weren't at the school library after all. After what had happened to Zamila, our parents had become stricter on rules, for example, never allowing us to leave the house unaccompanied by an adult. The only way we could leave that day was to tell our parents that we were going to the school library, where only students were allowed, and as I was young enough to pass for a student, I could go with Kushi...that way, she wouldn't be alone, or so I told my parents.

Khala said, "We sent Abdul to the school to pick you up, but you weren't there."

Amma asked with her teary gray eyes, "Where were you?"

Abba, who let a book slip out of his hands and fall to the floor, asked, "How did you get home?"

Their disappointed remarks and interrogation flew past us in slow-motion. Kushi ran to the bathroom and we heard her gag and vomit.

"Give her time," I begged Khala and Khalu. "She'll tell you everything." My calves suddenly lost their firmness and I found myself dizzy and leaning against the wall for support.

Khala yelled, "Zulekha! Abdul! Get our girls some water!"

I heard the television on in the living room. It caught all of our attention. There was breaking news and live coverage of Josh being arrested. Our parents recognized him, so they scurried over to the living room, where they watched the news intently. This also meant that they

346

watched us make our way past the pestering news reporter and into a car with Ishitha.

Kushi had just come out of the bathroom to see our parents gawking at us. We held hands as we approached them. Kushi told her parents about how Josh came into her life and how he tormented her every day. She confessed that she lied about him to protect her parents from his wrath, from his parents' wrath. She revealed that the only reason she accepted Salim's engagement was to escape her stalker.

"I'm sorry I didn't tell you the truth," She said. "I apologize, but I cannot marry Salim. It wouldn't be fair to him or to his family if I did; my heart wouldn't be in it. They deserve better. And I understand this puts you in a tough position, that your reputation will be...."

Before Kushi could finish her sentence, Khala wrapped her arms around her and sobbed. Kushi's tears joined the stream. Khalu wrapped his arms around both of them.

Khalu said, "Tough position? Us? Look at what you've been through! I am so sorry I wasn't there to listen to you, to help you. What kind of a man am I not to have been there?!"

Khala blubbered, "I am so sorry that I was blind to all of this; you've suffered too much, all alone, my dear, dear girl and it's all my fault!"

"Abba, Amma…," Kushi said, her face buried in between his neck and shoulder. "It's not your fault. You did nothing wrong. I made the mistake of not understanding how much you would have been there for me had I told you earlier. And Abba…I want to become an architect like you."

"Of course! You can be anything you want to be, my girl!" I was positive of that. I could already see Kushi and I holding hands and dancing again under the coconut palms, but this time, we would finally decipher their whispers of hopes and dreams. They would nudge us to start climbing the ladder of a rainbow to see what awaited us at the other end of it.

"Amma," Kushi struggled to say in between sniffs, "I want to use the English you taught me to do good in this world."

"Anything you dream of, you do it, okay?"

My parents and I teared up, watching them. I felt I owed them an apology too. "I'm sorry, Amma and Abba, for hiding all of this from you...."

"It's okay, my brave little girl," Amma said. "We're just happy that you're both safe, aren't we, Shah?"

"Yes, Amita, but...Asha..." Abba added. "Don't you ever dare keep something LIKE THIS a secret from us again!"

I nodded firmly.

"So, this is what you meant about finding the 'beautiful' in the 'ugly?!'" Amma said.

I replied, "After all of this, I realized that there is nothing beautiful about the ugliness we have gone through, but I am confident that there is a beauty *surrounding* it…even *beyond* it."

"Actually, finding beauty *beyond* all of this ugliness definitely sounds like an excellent plan," Amma said, and we hugged. Abba joined in. My chin nestled on Amma's shoulders as I closed my eyes. When I opened them, I saw a gruesome green face staring at me from the top of a mahogany coffee table. It was on the cover of a book with Bengali words in the title. I could not read Bengali, but I guessed what was written. *Frankenstein?* I asked nobody in particular. The surprises in this land kept coming. "Oh, that's my copy; it's been on my bookshelf for years," Khalu replied. "When I saw you reading it, I remembered I had it!"

"This is yours? In Bengali? Have you read it?" I asked.

"Yes."

Just as the first time I arrived at the house and saw Khalu reading *my* copy of *Frankenstein*, I analyzed his facial expression, still unable to read it. So, I had to ask him, "What did you think...about the story?"

He looked up toward the ceiling as if to recapture his thoughts that had escaped into the air years ago. Once he had gathered them from the archives of his mind, he said, "Such clever words to sum up the world."

I smiled. "Mary Shelley was very clever, indeed."

Khalu wrapped his arms around me. Khala did the same. As they did this, I realized that the red sun had released its grasp from around me. Darkness peered through the window, but it no longer lurked; it was as if the sun had asked it to check up on us to make sure that Kushi and I were okay. In my parents' arms and then my aunt's and my uncle's, I no longer replayed the events of the day in my head; rather, I replayed the events of my childhood. I thought to myself, *If only the entire world were this lucky!*

That night, Kushi and I drank chai on the rooftop. Both of us were in our kaftans, our hair up in messy buns and we spoke to each other only through sighs and smiles. I figured that the day and its successful outcome had been so overwhelming that we felt like there were no words to truly describe our sensations at that very moment. One thing was for sure; I had gained a sister for life. After all, together, we achieved justice, *not* vengeance or…maybe, both? I then remembered another point made in *Frankenstein*, *All was again silent.* And that wasn't necessarily a bad thing; in fact, silence contributed to the construction of words.

CHAPTER 12

THE COCONUT PALMS

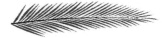

I tried shooing away the fear that had once stood in my way. I walked past it and stepped into the hospital room where Zamila had been staying. Kushi and I, although having attempted to prepare for this moment, knew that no amount of preparation could add up to handling whatever awaited us on the other side of that door.

"I am doing much better. Please come see me, my dear friends," I overheard Zamila struggling to say on the speaker during her phone conversation with Kushi.

So, we shoved fear aside and entered Zamila's room. She had this radiant smile that reached all the way up to her big brown eyes. She spread out her arms and let us fall into them.

Zamila looked frail and thin. We just blinked at her a few times before she said, "Oh, stop pitying me! I'm okay, just a few cuts and bruises, that's all."

That's all? "That's all" was this brave soul who had rescued us from Josh when he ambushed us at her parents' shop. "That's all" was this inspiration who literally stared down at the jaws of a monster and survived it. "That's all" was a humbleness we all strived for but could hardly achieve. "That's all" was this beauty in the face of everything ugly that she had been through.

"How are you both doing?" She asked us, sitting up a bit straighter.

354

Kushi helped her adjust her pillow before revealing her ringless fingers.

"What?! You're not getting engaged anymore?"

We smiled widely at her.

"But...I don't understand. How did this happen?"

Her searching eyes told us she had been oblivious to Josh's arrest. After all, she had been recovering.

"You mean Wings BD didn't tell you?" Kushi asked Zamila.

"Tell me about what?"

"We haven't told her yet," Officer Onthara, in her police uniform, peered in through the door. "We, at Wings BD, thought it'd be best if *you* both told her the good news."

"Well...?" Zamila asked. "What is it? What's the good news?" The words "good news" eagerly rolled off her tongue like it had been waiting there for way too long. "Josh is gone...for *good*," Kushi whispered as if saying it any louder could jinx it. But, there it was again, the word "good" except in another blissful context.

"What do you mean...he's gone?"

"He's been arrested," I clarified.

"Without bail," Officer Onthara added.

Words escaped our mouths in a silent procession. In other words, they were never spoken; rather, they reached our eyes and we cried. Kushi, Zamila and I sniffed and sobbed, wiping away our tears with our sleeves, all the while trying to smile at one another.

"How is it that you two look so gorgeous even when you cry?!" I asked.

They burst out laughing and our tears began to subside.

"Zamila..." Onthara began... "would you mind if I steal your friends away for a moment?"

"No, of course not! They're your friends too."

"You're such a sweetheart. You know that?!" Onthara said.

With that, we followed her outside of the room, where she asked us if we were still interested in volunteering at Wings BD and if we could begin our services that very day. Apparently, the girls were anxiously awaiting our arrival.

After we took turns feeding Zamila some homemade *kichri*, a soft and gooey mixture of lentils and rice, we joined Onthara in her police vehicle to make our way to the center.

As soon as we walked through the doors of Wings BD, a rainbow of balloons rained down on us. We were surrounded by applause on the part of the Wings BD members, the survivors, the personnel and the security. Estella Ambrosio, in a long white frock, welcomed us.

"We are celebrating a victory today and we applaud you both for your bravery."

"We applaud you all for your bravery every single hour of every single day!" Kushi said and she clapped until we all joined her.

Some people rubbed our backs, some shook our hands, and others nodded from a distance, mouthing or whispering, "Great job," "Congratulations," and "Thank you."

Estella led us into the garden, where Ishitha handed Kushi a tray of fruits.

"We'll start here today." Ishitha winked before leaving us in the garden.

"I'll leave you to it," Estella said and walked back inside.

Kushi and I watched the girls jump rope, swing and pass a ball around, among other activities. They then swarmed around us like hummingbirds in search of nectar. There was one girl who still sat by herself under a tree. Karishma was the 14-year-old girl who had been attacked by her stalker at the age of 13. Kushi and I both sat down beside her, keeping some distance in case she wanted alone time.

We got a closer look at Karishma's face that day. Whatever had been etched on her face were the marks of boldness, wisdom beyond years and ultimate survival. She had the boldness and wisdom to say "No" to her stalker. She survived a battle she had to fight all alone. Her face brought tears to our eyes. As soon as she looked up from the ground and noticed us, she began to cry too. *Was it wrong of us to get emotional in front of her? Was she upset we sat too close to her? Did she just want to be left alone? Did we shock her out of a deep contemplation?* Before I could continue my thoughts, Karishma made her way closer to Kushi, wrapped her arms around her neck and continued crying. Kushi held her tightly and nodded as if responding to something Karishma had whispered into her ear. She then pushed the girl's hair behind her ears to get a closer look at her face.

Kushi said, "You brave, brave girl. Don't thank me. Thank *you*!"

After eating fruits together with Karishma, in silence, we walked back inside the building, where I asked Kushi about what had happened.

"As we hugged, Karishma whispered, 'Thank you for catching him.'"

"You think Josh was the guy who attacked her?"

Kushi shrugged her shoulders. "I don't know. All we know is that I wasn't his first victim, so it's always a possibility."

"Come on, let's go home." On our way out, we met the honey-dew eyes of a familiar girl.

"Tanshara!" We yelled simultaneously before embracing her.

"I've been in touch with my family. They're doing well and they're happy, but they said they miss me. Estella arranged a meeting for us outside of the facility."

"Oh? Why not just bring them to Wings BD? They could see where you're staying, how your life is. Or, why not bring you home for a little while?" I asked her.

"It wouldn't be safe for her," Estella said from behind us. "We cannot risk her returning to a home that her ex-fiance knows the address to. And we have a lot of enemies out there; unfortunately, justice is not always served. So, we cannot risk revealing our girls' identities and shelter."

"Oh.... I understand," I said.

"That makes sense," Kushi said.

"I am very grateful to you, Estella," Tanshara said.

Estella smiled and combed her fingers through Tanshara's hair. She then turned to us. "I was just coming by to check up on you two. Did it go well out there?"

"Yes, actually. We had a great time with Karishma," Kushi said.

"Oh?" Estella said, surprised. "That is a breakthrough! You girls were made for this."

"Made…for what exactly?" I asked.

"For instilling hope in our girls by just being yourselves."

"I'm so happy to hear you say that, Estella. Actually, I would like to volunteer here for the remainder of my visit, but I was hoping you could write me a recommendation letter for college in return?"

She put her hand on her chest and took a step backward. "You don't have to…I understand you're busy…" I began rambling.

362

"It would be an honor!" She interceded and hugged me.

Afterward, Tanshara continued telling us how much she looked forward to seeing her family again after so many days. She also updated us on the friends she had made and new hobbies she had taken up. After a few minutes, we realized that it was time for us to go home and prepare for our next trip.

"Take care," I said on our way out. Turning to Kushi, I said, "Tanshara is just beaming, isn't she?"

"Yes, she is."

"Then, why do you look so sad, Sis?" I asked.

She kept her eyes on the ground as she spoke. "It's just that things will never again be the same for her, but at least she gets to achieve her dreams of becoming a doctor, and at least she's safer here." With those last two words, she met my eyes.

I nodded.

"Things will never be the same again, will they?" She repeated.

"You mean for Tanshara? Or for *you*?" I asked, leaving myself out of the question.

"Both."

"I remember when I first started learning how to ride a two-wheeled bicycle. Amma and Abba would push me along while holding on and then, one day, they just let go. When I realized that they were no longer holding on, I panicked and hit a lamp post, falling to the ground and scraping my knee pretty badly. Just three days later, I felt better, so I got back on that bike and tried to ride it by myself."

"So, basically, like Officer Onthara had once told us, we have to keep living life?" That night, we packed up some extra clothes for our trip to *dadabari*, which was my grandfather's village from my father's side. This time, we weren't escaping anything. We were just going on a vacation together, a day trip down memory lane. As I packed in my flower-printed maxi dress, towel and a few cookies, I got a flashback of a photo from my 12x12 leather album: it was a still shot of Abba feeding me mishti as we sat together on a canoe. I had also been wearing a flowery dress that day. Abba had matched me with a Hawaiian-style shirt. *He wouldn't be caught dead in that now!* I thought to myself and giggled. Just then, Abba walked in.

"Looking forward to our trip tomorrow?"

"Yup! Especially looking forward to riding a canoe with you."

Abba put his arm around my shoulder and squeezed it.

"Have I told you lately how much I love you?"

"Yes, but I'll take it as many times as it comes." I looked up at him and said, "I love you too, Abba."

"Get a good night's rest now!" He kissed my forehead and ruffled my hair before heading out.

I looked at the cover of *Frankenstein* and released a long sigh. Finally, I whispered, "You are the one monster I don't mind tagging along with me on this trip," and packed it in.

To get to dadabari, we had to drive across a red bridge overlooking the Surma River. On both sides of the bridge, below, I could see fishermen, in their lungis and neatly-wrapped rags around their heads, cast their nets into the water and gather in silver fish of varying sizes. A packed ferry glided across the water, leaving behind their temporary trails like rocks skidding across the water and leaving behind momentary ripples of the journey once taken. Close to the edge of the river were minuscule heads dipping in and out of the water; the children also splashed water at one another with their hands. Some women washed clothes and wrung them before placing them into a bucket. The Surma River was full of life and I longed to live it.

When we finally arrived at the village, we were welcomed by a large group of people circling us in front of the mud house. There was a rickshaw driver who offered us a ride around the village, free-of-charge. Of course, we suspected that deep down he wanted us to pay, which we would have done regardless. We kindly declined but gave him some money and a striped lungi as a gift. A little girl in pigtails and a frilly dress ran toward me. She gave me a red flower. I smiled and accepted it, patting her head. I tucked the flower's stem behind my ear to adorn my hair with it. The villagers did not seem to want to leave our home at dadabari. They basked in the sunshine the entire duration of our stay.

"They're just making sure we don't leave without giving out our money first," Kushi whispered to me.

I hit her arm.

"It's true," she exclaimed.

I rolled my eyes at her as we got ready for the tour. I took a backpack with me, in which I placed a towel, snacks and extra clothes in case I decided to bathe in the river.

Along the way, we saw children chasing chickens and chicks, a little girl carrying her sibling on her hip, a couple of boys playing cricket beneath a banyan tree and some cows grazing. At the river, we noticed a man in a lungi and purple shirt standing at the edge of a canoe. Abba greeted him and waved Kushi and me over.

"We are going to ride this canoe together," he said.

Sitting in the canoe, I noticed Kushi's hair flying in the wind as she looked off into the distance. It seemed like an anchor had been lifted off Kushi's back so that she could set sail. I took in a deep breath, let my fingers glide across the water and closed my eyes to feel the sunlight massaging my forehead. "So this is what it feels like to be carefree!" I said out loud to myself.

Kushi and Abba laughed at my comment. Abba came onto my side of the canoe, put his arm around me, and told Kushi to snap a photograph of us. Back on shore, Amma, Khala and Khalu were sunbathing on a blanket on the ground. I sat down next to Amma and continued reading *Frankenstein*. After what felt like the perfect amount of relaxation time, we wrapped everything up and headed back to the house for dinner before our van journey back to the city. Just as we stepped outside of the mud house, a crowd of villagers barricaded our way to the van we had rented just for this trip. Kushi was right. They *were* waiting for us to pass out charity money. Fortunately, we had come prepared with a trunk full of gifts and purses full of cash.

The same little girl who had given me the red flower tugged at my dress and asked, "Do you have a present for me?" I took out a little box of bangles just her size and handed it to her. She smiled a semi-toothless smile and I couldn't help but pinch her cheek before kissing it *goodbye*.

Just as our van pulled out, the little girl started yelling and running after it.

"Abba, stop the car! I think the girl is trying to tell us something."

I rolled down the window. Panting, she gave me a coconut. "They...they wanted me to give this to you."

"They?" I accepted the coconut. "Thank you."

I rolled the window back up and as the van started rolling again, I couldn't help but wonder, *what did the girl mean by "they?" Did she mean the other villagers? Did she mean her family? Did she mean the coconut palms?* I smiled, thinking about the latter.

That night, I sipped on some fresh coconut water while browsing through My Little Tanzanite journal for notes from the day's trip to dadabari. With that, I began writing my blog entry:

I had been trying to get to know Bangladesh on a whole new level. I came here expecting to just meet relatives and enjoy the landscape and the weather. I came here expecting a normal vacation, a home away from home. And I did! Moreover, I found a sister in my cousin, I made friends with strangers, I ended up confiding in the red sun as much as I did in the rain, I learned how to communicate with coconut palms and I met a snake charmer whom I envied! Bangladesh is, indeed, a magical place. I rode a canoe through the Surma River, read a book at its edge, tread farmlands past animals and people alike, fought night creatures in the village and shopped at bazaars in the city. I met a female police officer whose bravery could spread its wings and swoop you right up under them. I met a female leader who could rescue you from anything by sweeping you up onto her motorcycle and riding off into the night. I met many, many girls my age and even younger who had battled and survived darkness and found a light that beams so brightly throughout their bodies and into the world until bravery becomes contagious.

Amma taught me that there is so much beauty in the ugliness of this world. We just have to look hard enough to find it. Someone else told me that we just have to experience it all to live with it and then continue living beyond that experience.

When my trip to Bangladesh ends, this land and I will part as friends. The first words Khala uttered to me when I arrived at the house were, "As long as you are here, this is your home." And I plan on returning to it, inshAllah, which is Arabic for "God willing."

To accompany the post, I uploaded a photograph of Abba and me on the canoe and a photograph of the little girl who gave me the red flower and coconut. With that, I clicked *publish.*

CHAPTER 13

THE BEAUTIFUL

My friends surprise-visited me with "Welcome Back" balloons and a chocolate cheesecake. I looked over at Amma, who winked at me. I figured it was definitely she who had invited them over. She probably saw me moping about and swiping through our digital photographs from our trip to Bangladesh. I needed to land...I mean, *really, truly* land back in the Bronx. Amma probably thought this would help. I did too. Rachel talked about how for Christmas, her parents gifted her with a special set of tires for her bike just so she could ride it in the snow. Angel showed me the latest Online game she had figured out all the secret codes to. Maria gave me a makeover with the Christmas present she got, an expensive makeup kit with the face of a celebrity on it. And Noreen told me about her rowdy cousins who had visited from Dallas, Texas. When it came to *my* turn to tell them about my trip to Bangladesh, I showed them the photographs, telling them about what a wonderful time I had at the villages and at the bazaar with my cousin. I left the part about stalkers and child marriage out of it. I carried those moments like my own shadow, dragging them behind me everywhere I went; it felt like something extremely contagious, and I did not want my friends to catch it. However, I did ask them for one thing that I felt I needed the most before fully landing my head and my heart back in America: "Group hug!" After my friends had left our apartment, my morbid thoughts took me back into flight mode. I so badly wanted to escape them, so I thought that reading a book would help. I thought back to Mary Shelley's words from *Frankenstein*, except this time, I made the mistake of reading the *entire* quote: *"All was again silent; but his words rung in my ears. I burned with rage to pursue the murderer of my peace, and precipitate him into the ocean. I walked up and down my room hastily and perturbed, while my imagination conjured up a thousand images to torment and sting me."* I quickly realized it wasn't entirely true what Ishitha had said to Kushi and me about how eventually, we would let go of what had happened. We let go to some degree, yes, but not *completely* and I couldn't help but feel that there was some purpose in that...that somehow those experiences had shaped us in some...positive way?

After reading the dreadful quote, I spent hours passionately writing the first essay draft on my literary analysis of *Frankenstein*. I began with the surface of his creation, *"His face was wrinkled into contortions too horrible for human eyes to behold."* And then, I went deeper into his character just as I had spent time getting to know him. After having written my draft, I just smiled, thinking about how ironic it was that one of my closest companions in Bangladesh had been *Frankenstein,* a fictitious monster of sorts, just as my cousin and I had been chased by a non-fiction one.

On my way back to school, the confidence I felt in my essay was not as overwhelming as the paranoia following closely behind me. I found myself constantly looking over my shoulders, so when I felt a tap on my shoulder, I gasped in panic.

"Woah, it's just me," Noreen said.

"Hi," I dragged out, looking over *her* shoulder.

She turned around to see what I was looking at... *nothing.*

Noreen brushed her fingers through her bangs and asked, "Is it horrible?"

"Eh?"

"My Texas cousins told me that bangs would suit me."

We walked side-by-side. "They do! They look great on you!"

"Whew. Thanks. Cute top, by the way!"

She referred to my turquoise-colored kurti ornate with white threadwork embroidery. "Thanks! My aunt gifted me with it as a kind of farewell present."

A moment of silence passed between us.

"So…." She drew out.

"So…." I drew out.

"What was that back there?" She asked.

"What was what back where?" . "Oh, come on! I know you, Asha. I noticed there's something different about you since you came back from Bangladesh. Something's changed...."

We stared at each other for a few seconds before I heard the vroom of a vehicle and pulled Noreen to follow me into an alleyway. When the noise faded, I puffed out a sigh of relief.

"Okay, you're officially freaking me out," she said.

I noticed my shadow against the brick wall, growing taller and taller before it completely engulfed me. I held back tears as I confessed to Noreen that her suspicion about this change in me was correct. "Okay, let's talk." As we continued on our way to school, I told her everything about what had happened to my cousin and me. In a way, talking about it shrunk my shadow a bit.

Of course, the only person with whom I could truly share everything with was Kushi. We communicated often. We tried to comfort one another, knowing fully well that words were not enough to help us get over it all. So, we set off on yet another mission, but a less risky one than "Stalk the Stalker." Kushi continued volunteering at Wings BD and I joined the volunteering program at a local domestic violence shelter for women and children.

"Abba and I are working together at his architectural firm, designing a row of independent houses for the women and girls at Wings BD," Kushi had said over the phone one day.

"That sounds like a dream come true for an aspiring architect such as yourself!" I replied, tucking myself under the covers.

"Well…" she said in a quivering voice. I could tell by her tone that she was teary-eyed. "It was Abba's birthday gift to me. He asked me what I wanted and this was exactly what I needed." And by the word "needed," she really meant it, and I...*understood* it.

379

Ever since I occupied myself with the shelter, I looked over my shoulders less and the loud sounds of vehicles became more irritating than intimidating. I played board games and had movie nights with these women and children. I also participated in a program helping high schoolers prepare for the SATs and apply to college. Sooner than I knew it, I found myself standing in front of the mirror in that blue cap and gown with the golden honors sash across my chest. I took a selfie and sent it to Kushi.

Underneath the gown, I wore a long, white, net dress with beige heels. Yet, something was missing.

There was a knock on the door.

I opened it to see Amma, who said, "Here's the blush pink lipstick you wanted to borrow."

"Perfect! Thanks!"

"Nervous?" She asked.

"A little, but it helps having you and Abba there. I just wish...."

"You wish Kushi were here, too?"

I nodded.

"I told you that you'd both get to that point someday, the point where you become more like sisters than ever. Now, you know how I feel every time there's a big moment in my life and my sister isn't here for me to share it with. I especially missed my sister on the day when you were born. You are the biggest blessing in my life and I am forever grateful for that. So proud of you, Shuna. My little Asha...not so little anymore."

Choking back tears, I replied, "You and Abba are the biggest blessings in my life," followed by "*Alhumdulillah*," which was Arabic for "Thanks to God." I hugged Amma, who also had on a long white maxi dress, her shoulders draped over with a golden shawl.

"Can I join this hug fest?" Abba chimed in. He wore a suit.

After the "hug fest," Abba looked at his watch and hurried us out.

Before we headed to the graduation ceremony, however, I took one long look at the framed words on my desk: *Whoever treads the path toward knowledge, Allah will make easy for him/her the path to Paradise.* Then, I turned to my parents and said, "I just have to make one stop on the way."

The brick building where the shelter was located had a courtyard in the center of it. Rose bushes, lilies and tulips were already in bloom, surrounding a fountain. As I walked past it, I heard the tapping of my heels echo from wall to wall and perfectly in tune with the bouncing of a ball. I waved *hello* to the kids passing that ball around. As I walked into the shelter, I ran into a mother pushing her baby carriage outside.

"Bipa, hi!" I said. "How's little Shams doing?" I asked her about her baby.

"Shams is looking forward to getting some Vitamin D today, aren't we?!" She asked in a smothering baby tone. She then pushed some of her brunette curls away from her face as if to get a better look at me through her sunglasses.

Meanwhile, I squished a little squeaky toy to make Shams giggle.

"How could I forget that you're graduating today?! You make sure you come back right after so you get your present!"

"Oh no, please, you don't have to get me anything!"

"I won't hear of it! I am on my way out now and your present will be waiting here for you right after that."

"You really don't have to...."

"I want to!"

I giggled. "Is Laura in?" I asked about the receptionist.

"When have you ever known her not to be in?!" Bipa said, laughing, before setting off for her walk with her baby.

Upon entering, Laura said, "Oh! Now, look at that load of gorgeousness!" She cackled. "Let me see you do a twirl!"

I twirled for one of the most energetic and friendly people I had in my life. "Thank you, Laura. You always know how to make me feel so special."

"Oh girl, you are special and we are lucky to have you in our lives! Don't know how we'd survive these past six months without you volunteering here!"
She spread out her arms and wrapped them around me.

"I don't know how I'd survive without this place." I felt like those words had been resting on the tip of my tongue the entire time I had been volunteering at the shelter. Finally, the words were out and free.

"Hello, Mia," I said to a 17-year-old redhead passing by.

"Oh wow, Asha! You look incredible!" She ran her fingers up and down my golden sash. "Smarty pants!"

"Thank you! This will be you next year!"

"I sure hope so," she solemnly replied.

"I know so!" I said, holding her hands tightly in mine.

She smiled.

"Now you go on, grab that diploma by the hips and do the cha-cha-cha with it," Laura said, swaying from side – to –side and I couldn't help but laugh at her beautiful Latino spirit.

The world could use more people like Laura. After her brief dance performance, she took out her phone to take a picture of me.

"You and Mia get in for a selfie!" I said.

There was a loud noise in the kitchen. I could hear the angry screams of two women.

"You guessed right," Laura said, reading my thoughts written all over my face. "They're at it again."

Candice and Juanita were frenemies. Both came to the shelter around the same time. They have a lot in common, including their temper. Laura said my presence was calming for them, so she literally pushed me in the middle of one of their arguments once. I just sat down and watched the two before they asked me who I was and what I was doing there.

I wouldn't say my presence was as calm for them as much as it was a simple distraction.

"Ladies!" I said as I walked into the kitchen. "Thank you for making my graduation day as exciting as ever!" I looked at blond-haired Candice, then at fiery-redheaded Juanita and finally at the broken glass on the floor. They had clearly been arguing *again* over whose turn it was to reluctantly empty the dishwasher. As soon as they noticed my outfit, they both ran to me and hugged me.

"Congratulations!" Juanita said.

"We are so proud of you!" Candice said.

"Aw, look at her…." Juanita said. Both just stared at me up and down in the most adoring manner before their eyes glazed up.

"Oh, stop it, you two! You're going to make *me* cry!" I hadn't realized how much this day had also meant to them. The two, who had been separated from their husbands after only having been married less than a year, had once dreamed of settling down and having their own children. They had once expressed their dreams of holding their children's hands before letting go of them on their first day of school, watching them grow up, teaching them how to ride bikes and attending their graduation ceremonies.

"What are you doing here? You should be walking on stage and grabbing your diploma!" Candice said.

"Well, if I had it my way, I would have ALL of you there watching me do exactly that! But, since that can't happen…."

"You came to us because we can't come to you," Juanita said before balling. Candice joined her. I grabbed tissues for both of them, before I needed one, myself.

On my way out, I noticed lines of women and children waiting to congratulate me. I suddenly felt time warped back to Wings BD. I hugged every single one, thinking about how these individuals had faced so much ugliness in their lives but were living in the beauty beyond all of that ugliness. I wondered if my presence had made any impact on helping them get to the other side of the rainbow.

My phone bleeped. I looked down at the screen to read Kushi's response to the graduation selfie I had sent her.

"You look beautiful," she wrote. "Congratulations, my dear sister."

THE END.

ACKNOWLEDGEMENTS

I am grateful to my parents, Rana and Sajjad, who encouraged my dreams of pursuing English and becoming a published author.

I appreciate my husband, Jony, who told me that as long as I am determined, I can do anything; and reminds me to celebrate the little things in life.

This book is also for my hope (my asha) and brother, Robin (Ryhan), who I can still feel holding my hands every letter I type; may your soul rest in peace, may all your dreams finally come true in Jannah and may we meet again there, Ameen.

Thank you, "jnrst" and "cuzzos" for your constant support. You are all sisters to me.

Thank you, my mother-in-law, Akhtar, and father-in-law, Nurul, with whom I revisited Bangladesh after years since my childhood; it was an inspirational journey.

Thank you, my cousin-in-law, Sharmin, to whom I read my very first draft of this story.

Thank you, my friends who took the time to read my manuscript and gave me feedback: Sana, Musart, Nazhah, Katharina and Kamrul.

Thank you, Papatia (H.) of Djarabi Kitabs Publishing, who called me "Sis" during my publishing journey and still does.

ABOUT THE AUTHOR

Rumki Chowdhury was born in Bangladesh and grew up in the USA. She has also lived in the UK and Sweden. With an MA in English Literature from The Queen Mary University of London and a BA in English Writing from The William Paterson University of New Jersey, her literary experiences expand from journalism to publishing companies like Simon and Schuster Inc., Pearson Higher Education Publishing, *The Herald Newspaper* and *The Record Newspaper*. Rumki's previous book publications include *So Complicated*: A "he vs. she" romantic comedy/women's fiction that won Honorable Mention at The New York Book Festival, Second Place at UK's The Wishing Shelf Award and Finalist for Humor at The Pacific Writer's Award. She has also authored *Her Feet Chime*, the first and only Bangladeshi version of a Cinderella story written in English. Moreover, 100% of profits from her poetry book, *Unveiled*, go to helping the Rohingya refugees in Bangladesh via Restless Beings. Another poem was published in *Hijri*, a collection of stories by various authors. Her memoir was also published in *Your Story with Musart*, a collection of inspirational stories by various authors. *Secrets in the Wind* is her first work of fiction/thriller in the YA department. In addition, Rumki provides her own editing services to authors and various media including Bengalis of New York, The World Hijab Day Organization and Hayati Magazine. She is an active blogger on writing advice via www.rumki.com and Social Media @rumkitheauthor.

392